Praise for Jo Mazelis

Ritual, 1969

In this fine collection, Jo Mazelis proves herself mistress of the short-story form. A selection of unflinching stories move across time and landscape, linked by the revealing details of human behaviour, the voices of the unloved and an unsettling imagination. Haunting, beautifully crafted fictions.

Cathy Galvin, director, www.thewordfactory.tv

With prose that is as beautiful and harsh as her stories, Jo Mazelis has produced a string of tales full of yearning and loss. Her characters, mainly women, young and old, are linked through passions misplaced and longings unmet – or else traduced. But there's nothing wistful about *Ritual 1969*: the writing is precision-modulated, witty, barbed. It's as refreshing as a cold shower, and uplifting as a levitation.

Marina Benjamin, *The Middlepause*

Mazelis writes about the repressed desires·and casual cruelties of suburban life with an acute sensitivity that lends these stories an almost dreamlike, even Gothic quality. Imagine if *Carrie* had been set in 1970s Swansea and filmed by Mike Leigh rather than Brian de Palma and you're getting close to describing the atmosphere of a collection that is marked by a particularly British sense of melancholia and surrealism.

Ritual, 1969 is an unapologetically feminist work that relays the pitfalls of a troubled journey from school to womanhood with considerable depth and artistry. Mazelis writes in the tradition of Woolf, Plath and Carter, and does not feel out of place in their company. Like those writers she takes apparently mundane, everyday dramas and reveals them to be extraordinary and defining moments in an individual's lifetime.

John Lavin, *The Lonely Crowd, Wales Arts Review*

As in her previous short-story collections, Jo Mazelis in this new book proves herself to be a virtuoso of the genre. As usual, she sees with the eyes of those marginalised by power – children, servants, women. But there's nothing worthy or sentimentally victimised about her writing, which is always alert to the oddly resonant detail, even the grotesque, in every existence.

Indeed, many of these tales have a gothic or supernatural cast... They refuse cheap consolation – the style is bare, if beautifully crafted, and several stories, such as 'The Murder Stone', concern the terrible minor-seeming errors and misunderstandings that can blight the rest of a life. But they are at the same time the opposite of downbeat or heartless, are charged with ironic empathy, reminding us again and again of the poetry and sheer strangeness of human existence.

John Goodby

Georgina and Charlotte are Siamese twins… *Ritual, 1969* broods on the strange conjunctions and fateful symmetries that shape the lives of women who seem fated never to be in control of their own individual stories. Only gradually do we realize that those stories themselves are silently interconnected, their characters recurrent… The result is a powerful double-take on female experience.'

M. Wynn Thomas

Significance; winner of the Jerwood Fiction Uncovered Award 2015

'Quite unlike any literary crime novel that I have read before, seriously… It is rather like Mazelis has taken a box filled with all the crime novel/thriller tropes and really shaken it up to see what can be done outside the box…

There is also a much deeper level to the novel than just an enthralling and entertaining, and it should be said beautifully written (you can tell Mazelis is a poet, the writing is lyrical yet has real pace) and crafted, read. From the title you would imagine that the novel is about the significance of a murder and of course it is, yet it is also about many other significances; the significance we give ourselves and others, the significance we are given, the significance of tiny details or moments and how they can change everything. It is also a book that is very much about perception, the things we notice and the things that we don't.'

Simon Savidge, Jerwood Fiction Uncovered judge

Significance is a novel that toys with and interrogates the mystery fiction genre itself, often reproaching the stereotypes created there … the introduction of new characters continues way past the point any creative writing tutor or manual would advise an aspiring writer to stop. Yet Mazelis makes each and every one of them seem vital and engaging… With *Significance*, Mazelis has set her novel-writing bar at a breathtaking height.

Rachel Trezise, *Agenda*

With its intricate plotting and many-layered narrative *Significance* turns out to be completely engrossing. There's a crime but this isn't a crime novel: it's a study in human nature and the way we interact and observe each other… It's all beautifully done.

A gripping first novel, thoroughly deserving of its prize.

A Life in Books

Jo Mazelis has a wonderful elliptical approach to her writing – nothing is as it seems. What sets out to be a straightforward thriller succeeds in becoming a seductive narrative, transforming itself into a delicate maze of events, interspersed by arresting characters brushed in with the touch of a seasoned writer… It is a cool and sophisticated look at human interaction, loving, violent and inexplicable simultaneously. There are no neat answers, no predictable plot structures. *Mazelis* evades the stereotypical – yet her characters are recognisable as they cope with the bewildering situations they find themselves in. Quite a tour de force for a debut novelist.

Sarla Langdon The Bay

A literary crime novel in which the 'whodunnit' and even the 'whydunnit' is less significant than the mystery of who the victim is (or who any of us are)… *Significance* is written with admirable storytelling skill that weaves captivating narrative tension, poetic density and exploration of ideas. Further enjoyment is provided by an acute sense of place … and by the precision and awareness of the power of language…

Valerie Sirr, Wales Arts Review

I was gripped from the first chapter to the unexpected ending and cannot recommend this book highly enough.

Leslie Williams The Bay

Circle Games (2005)

Mazelis' latest collection of short stories is permeated with an undercurrent of barely suppressed unease in which the ordinary is transformed into something altogether more disturbing. Capturing the frequently shaky basis on which her characters interrelate, Mazelis explores love in its various manifestations, together with the complicated games it causes people to play, both with themselves and with one another…

Mazelis has produced an imaginatively written collection which draws strength from the all-too-human flaws and weaknesses of its characters.

Anna Scott, New Welsh Review

Circle Games leaves you disturbed and dislocated – with a feeling that all is not quite right, that there's an itch you can't locate. Which is quite as it should be. Jo Mazelis' short stories are, on the surface, concerned with the everyday – for the most part small slices of life that one is quick to identify with, where something is always familiar. But there is no sense of ease, everything falls just short of closure, and her images return to you again and again – the literary equivalent of looking at a Paula Rego painting. Highly recommended.

Amazon review

Diving Girls (2002)

Misunderstandings and miscommunications, and the danger of superficial masks… This theme of penetrating surface exteriors in relationships among both family members and society's outsiders is constant throughout this collection, where initial appearances belie a contradictory reality. The insignificance of images and slogans is constantly revealed. The intricacies of relationships within families are laid bare in a number of the stories, and especially the tensions between parents and children.

Liz Saville, Gwales.com

Ritual, 1969

For Ben, Nico and Megan

Ritual, 1969

Jo Mazelis

Seren is the book imprint of
Poetry Wales Press Ltd
57 Nolton Street, Bridgend, Wales, CF31 3AE
www.serenbooks.com
Facebook: facebook.com/SerenBooks
Twitter: @SerenBooks

ISBNs
Pback – 978-1-78172-305-0
Ebook – 978-1-78172-307-4
Kindle – 978-1-78172-306-7

A CIP record for this title is available from the British Library.

The publisher acknowledges the financial assistance of the Welsh Books
Council.

Printed in the Czech Republic
by Akcent Media Ltd.

Cover: Self-portrait, London, 1984, Jo Mazelis

O Rose thou art sick.
The invisible worm,
That flies in the night
In the howling storm:

Has found out thy bed
Of crimson joy:
And his dark secret love
Does thy life destroy.

William Blake 'The Sick Rose'

'Children are taught revenge and lies in their very cradles.'
Mary Wollstonecraft, *Thoughts on the Education of Daughters*

CONTENTS

LEVITATION, 1969

Rising up in the air, the dead girl feels ... dead. Her eyes are closed; for a moment she has forgotten everything. She is dead.

Then alive again. They have set her down on the concrete wall and the ceremony is over. They do not misuse the levitation game – weeks and even months go by and they don't do it or even think of doing it – as if it's a dream that occasionally recurs, but is forgotten when the sleeper wakes. Then at some point in time it stops. They never perform the act of levitation again.

The game arrived in their lives after the circle games of 'The Farmer's in His Den' and 'Oranges and Lemons' had fallen away, but before the long passage of no-games-at-all enveloped them forever.

The reign of levitation is also that of puberty. Is it not said that pubescent girls and boys, those on the cusp of change are the most vulnerable and attractive to the spirit world? That in homes where poltergeists are active there is usually in residence a child in their early teens?

The dead girl (who is not really dead) lives in a home with such a poltergeist. Objects are broken; china smashed into many pieces, the old black Bakelite telephone – the one whose weight and heft suggested unalienable permanence – is suddenly and mysteriously transformed. It catches her eye when she comes home from school. It is in its usual place by the front door, but something is different. She looks

13

closely, sees an intricate pattern of lines and cracks all over it and, in places, evidence of glue. The phone has somehow been broken into a hundred jagged shards and then someone (she knows who) has painstakingly, with his Araldite and magnifier, tweezers and spent matches, put it back together again.

Such an event should come up in conversation in a small family like theirs but no one says a word. The destruction was the work of an angry spirit; the reconstruction was performed by her father, who is often to be found with a soldering iron in his hand, or a pair of needle-nose pliers, an axe or hammer.

One autumn day years before, she came across him in the garden, tending a fire of fallen leaves. Such a fire is always an event for a child of eight or nine so she stands at a safe distance to watch how he rakes and prods it, how the flames change colour from red to blue to white to yellow.

He stirs his pyre of smoking leaves; the centre gives way and something hidden is revealed: first, brown paper that flares away to black tissuey fragments, then white fabric pads, some folded in upon themselves, others that boldly show their faces with their Rorschach test ink blots of red and rust-coloured blood. Her mother's blood, her mother's sanitary towels – which belong to the secret places of locked bathrooms – are out here being burned by her father in the front garden of their home where any neighbour or passerby might see.

Behind her father is the oak tree and behind that the ivy-covered low stone wall and in the earth just in front is a bamboo pole that she has topped with a bird's skull – a totem she had made to ward off danger.

This was long ago, before the poltergeist and the angry

words that echo through the house late at night to infiltrate her dreams, turning them into nightmares.

One day her mother came home from the shops and announced she had found a lucky charm. She reached into her coat pocket and pulled out a tiny little hand made from cheap nickel-plated metal. The thumb was tucked into the palm and so were the two middle fingers, leaving just the index and little finger standing proudly erect.

'Aren't those meant to represent the Devil's horns?' the girl said, not knowing where such knowledge came from.

Her mother's eyes widened in horror and she threw the charm from her hand into the empty sink. Later she took it into the garden and was gone for some time. When she came back into the house she looked tired and frightened.

'I tried to smash it,' she told her daughter. 'Then I tried to burn it. It's indestructible; it must have been made by the Devil.'

Now the girl is eleven years old and goes to big school where as the littlest, lightest one among her friends she always plays the dead girl.

'This is the law of levitation...'

There is no greater pleasure than the moment when the other girls lift her high into the air. Her body remains absolutely straight; at no place, either at one leg or at her head, does a weaker girl fail to do the magic and she seems to almost float upward. No one laughs and the dead girl's eyes remain closed. She believes. All of them believe.

Her body is still that of a child while all around her the other girls are changing or have already changed into women. After sports they are meant to strip and go into the communal shower, all of them naked together, sixteen or seventeen girls, most of whom have never done such a thing before. None of them are muddy or even sweaty; a half-hour of netball is hardly an exertion, especially after the enforced stillness of sitting at a desk listening to an array of voices droning on about Pythagoras and the tributaries of the Nile and flying buttresses and Beowulf and blanket stitch and the creaming method for making cakes. She and a few other girls run to the showers with their towels wrapped carefully around themselves, then after splashing a little water over their heads and feet they run back to the changing area again.

The poltergeist at home is getting worse. Last night after she had gone to bed he tore the television set from the stand and jumped on it. She doesn't know if he was careful to switch it off and take out the plug first. Probably, as he's always telling them all to do just that.

She has dark circles under her eyes. She is thin and (though no one knows this) anaemic. She does not do her homework. Every time her parents ask if she has any she says 'no' or claims that she did it on the bus.

She is like a fallen leaf caught up in a strong gust of wind. She has no locomotion. In biology Mr Thomas had taught them that as seeds have no locomotion they must find other means of dispersal, hence the helicopter wings of sycamore seeds.

In the playground, from behind her, something hard and knobbly is laid upon her head. This may be the start of another interesting game, but when she turns, she sees that the hand belongs to a girl she does not really know, a girl who gives her a smile that is glittering with malice. She has only just understood that the object on the top of her head is a curled fist when its partner arrives to smash it down. It is meant to be like a raw egg breaking on her head, but it is far more painful than that. It hurts as much as if the girl had just straightforwardly punched her. It is instead a complex violence that is nearly impossible to react to. It is delivered in the guise of a joke, but the message is menace.

She grimaces with pain and her eyes water.

Don't cry, whatever you do, don't cry.

Weakly she smiles, then grimaces again, this time comically, exaggerating her expression in the hope they will appreciate her humour. This is a tactic that usually works, but not now, not with this girl and her silent, sneering sidekick.

Instead they point right at her, index fingers dangerously close to poking out an eye, and laugh jeeringly, artificially. WHA HA HA!

Then as quickly as they had arrived they are gone and whatever *that* was is over.

At around two in the afternoon it grows unnaturally dark, nearly as black as night. The teacher has switched on the overhead lights, and attempts to keep their attention on the lesson, but beyond the big plate-glass window the distant hills and far-off steelworks are the dramatic backdrop to a spectacular performance given by the weather. Grey-black clouds fill the sky and the air is charged with electricity. The children can barely keep their eyes from the window; the teacher raps the wooden board-duster sharply on her desk creating a cloud of chalk dust, but their attention is snagged by a greater primordial force.

'Never mind the storm, we have work to do. Now, look at your books, what is the meaning of…'

A flash of lightning draws a collective gasp from the children, loud enough to cut the teacher off in mid-sentence. Seconds later, distantly, there is the rumble of thunder.

'Woah!' one boy cries and abandons his chair to run to the window, and then nearly all of the children are by the window staring outside, their eyes wide with wonder. Lightning zigzags down again and again on the black shrouded hills; magnesium-white veins that burn onto the retina, while the tin-tray thunderclaps grow louder and more insistent.

Unlike the others, the dead girl stays in her seat. She can see just as well from there as from the scrum of elbows and sharp knees and bony heads that are ducking and dancing and roaring by the window. She is no less moved than the others, no more obedient than they, but she has withdrawn into herself. She is a pair of green eyes looking out at the turning world as the leaf of her body is taken there, or battered by that, or torn by this.

Seconds pass and finally she no longer wants to remain in her seat; she wants to belong, to be like the other children, to break the rules like them, to press her face against the cold glass by the window and feel the thrum in her cheekbones as the sound waves batter and shake it.

'Children!' the teacher is saying. 'Calm down at once!'

The dead girl pushes back her chair. She wears a beatific smile as she stands and begins to take the few steps which will bring her to the window. She seems to glide forward, focusing her gaze on the distant hills. She does not see the teacher bearing down on her. She hears the tirade of words coming from the teacher's mouth, but they are as generalised as the thunder.

'I will not have this! I will not tolerate such insubordination in my classroom. Sit down! Sit down at once! YOU!'

The teacher catches her arm, wrenching it sideways, forcing her to turn. The older woman's face up close is terrifying, her expression almost insane with fury.

'How dare you!' she roars, then slaps the dead girl's left cheek. 'Stop grinning, child!' she adds, but the girl's smile has already gone and her face is blank once more.

She closes her eyes.

'She *is* dead,' the girl standing at her head says, and the voices travel around her prone body, echoes of what has been, of what is to come. Then they are lifting her, higher and higher, to waist level, then shoulder level, then above their heads, to the furthest reach of their upstretched arms and fingers. Then higher still and higher again until she is floating far overhead. Then finally, although the other girls shade their eyes and search the sky they can no longer see her. She's free.

CARETAKERS

'Human beings are 70 per cent water. The brain is roughly 85 per cent water...'

She is gazing at the lecturer trying to fight back a yawn. She is so tired her eyes are tearing up. She searches her bag, but no pen. Just a dried-up, electric-lime highlighter. She looks around at the students near her, mouths the word 'pen', makes a squiggle in the air to signify her want. Cold eyes study her, frown, then dismiss her as if she is merely a clown, a puppeteer whose hand is suddenly naked and meaningless.

She leans forward in her chair and stretches out to tap Lolly's shoulder. As he turns, she catches, from beneath her armpit, the strong scent of sweat. Lowers her arm quickly.

'Pen,' she whispers urgently.

Lolly raises his eyebrows, turns back, riffles in his bag then produces a biro. She has to lean over to take it. Her sweat is greasy smelling, like pork and onions.

When the lecture finishes just before lunch, she does not follow the other students to the refectory, but goes home to shower.

Last night she couldn't sleep. All because of the wet foot-prints she saw; running in a line from the bathroom to the fireplace in her bedroom. The footprints were far smaller than her own. Child-sized naked heel and toe marks, damp on the floorboards and carpet, quickly evaporating to nothing.

The other houses on her street are a mixture of 1930s

mock Tudor semis, new apartment blocks and terraced cottages. Hers is the oldest, a Georgian landowner's pile, double-fronted, whitewashed, tall sash windows and six bedrooms. She lives here alone, half ashamed of her good luck in possessing such a house, half afraid that it will somehow be taken from her, invaded, despoiled. She has lived there for over four months. Since September, when she moved in, disbelieving, everything she owned in an old suitcase and a black bin bag. Everything she owned – not forgetting the house and all its contents: the antique furniture, the mahogany and horsehair, the ivory and silks and ormolu, the oil paintings and watercolours, the butler's pantry with its silverware, its cut glass and Clarice Cliff tea sets.

The house was left to her by her great uncle. It was a slap in the face to his children and five grandsons, her own parents and his housekeeper (who may or may not have been his mistress for the preceding fifty years).

'Don't go and live in that awful house,' her mother said. 'Just sell it.' But it was near the college and she felt compelled somehow, duty-bound.

She puts her bag on the rosewood table in the hall and hangs her jacket on the coat-stand with its carved menagerie of real and mythical creatures, a stag, a unicorn, frogs and lizards with inlaid eyes of ebony, amber and jet. Kicks off her shoes at the base of the stairs and goes up, two steps at a time.

On the landing she stops and searches the floor for signs of footprints. Nothing. She draws closer and kneels to inspect the area for the barest trace of a dark or water-beaded mark.

She glances into her bedroom. Nothing there. Then

goes into the bathroom and locks it before disrobing. Turns on the ancient shower and steps under its spluttering, thundering water. Washes herself, then stands, turning this way and that, luxuriating in the liquid heat. She feels at peace. Cleansed and transcendent. Not reborn, but returned to the womb, to the state of being where there are no edges or boundaries. She lingers, eyes closed, hair plastered flat against her skull, down her back.

She does not go back to college that day. Or the day after that, a Friday. Spends hours curled up on the sofa, the TV on. Thinks that she could go on like this. Forever and forever. If she wasn't so lonely.

On Monday she goes back to college. No one has noticed her absence. They ignore her as before.

After the seminar, she goes to the refectory and does not, as she has in the past, attempt to sit at a table with her fellow students. But they, as bad luck would have it, occupy the table behind her. She can hear every tedious word of their conversation. None of which she wants to hear. Until…

'Did you hear about Lolly?'

'No. What?'

'He's just like, totally broke.'

'Really?'

'Yeah. His father's supposed to pay his rent. But he hasn't, so Lolly's being chucked out.'

'Oh my God!'

'So he owes like nearly a thousand, but his father won't help him and he can't go home.'

'What's he going to do?'

There is no audible answer to this, perhaps the speaker merely shrugged.

They change the subject. She stops listening. Finishes her food, gets up and walks away, very deliberately not looking at them. Someone laughs, perhaps at her.

She sees Lolly crossing the big hall, weaving between tables packed with students. He has a plate of chips and a white plastic cup of water. Nothing else. Lolly is a big guy, tall, broad-shouldered, but also overweight. His lumberjack shirt is crumpled and he looks like he needs a shave. Tucked away, near the fire exit is a narrow corridor with three small tables, he heads there and she follows. At one of the tables, sitting on a chair as if waiting for a companion is a large nylon rucksack, on the floor beside it are two carrier bags, and a sleeping bag. Lolly slumps into the seat opposite.

She pulls over a chair and sits.

'Lolly,' she says.

'Don't call me that.'

'But everyone…'

'My name is Lawrence.'

He averts his gaze and begins eating.

'So … someone said you were looking for a place…'

'Oh yeah? Well someone is talking out of their ass. OK?'

'Oh. I'm sorry. I heard that … and then here you are with your rucksack and this bag and…'

He looks her in the eye; his expression is flat, guarded. She waits. He says nothing.

'I was going to say. You know, if you're stuck. Between places? Then you could stay at mine. For a while. If you want…'

'For real? Are you for real?' A grin is starting to break out all over his face. He's handsome when he smiles.

'Yeah, for real.'

When their last lecture finished at three she and Lolly lin-

gered until the rest of the class drifted away, before setting
off together – him almost a giant, made even larger by his
huge rucksack. She, at least a head and a half shorter, had
to run every few paces to keep up with him.

They didn't talk. There was no conversational opening
which wouldn't have been painful for either; he didn't want
to talk about his father, she was ashamed of owning a big
Georgian house set in an acre of land, he did consistently
well at college, she was scraping along most of the time.
Everybody at college liked him, though he seemed to make
no effort to be liked, while she tried desperately to charm
and ingratiate herself, but got nowhere.

The Lolly/Lawrence thing was interesting, she thought
as they turned into her street, he hated being called Lolly
but said nothing. The man they all liked, Lolly, Big Loll,
Lolls who was tall and a tad overweight, but handsome and
affable, was their own invention. The jolly giant, he was
safe, good at walking home girls too drunk to look after
themselves.

In a similar fashion they must have created a version of
her that bore little resemblance to reality. This person was
spiky and mean, jealous of the other girls.

Maybe as she and Lawrence got to know one another
better they would have a conversation about this, and then
understanding everything about her, he would become her
envoy, making others see her in a whole new light.

As they began down the drive to the house, he gave no
sign of surprise at its majesty. But then he had no idea of
her relationship to the house, she might have been a live-
in skivvy for all he knew and lived in a caravan around the
back.

'Here it is.'

He stepped in and looked around.

She had almost stopped seeing how grand the hall was, but now she could see its magnificence reflected in his gaze.

'How many people live here?'

'Just me.'

'Just ... you?'

'I'm the caretaker.'

He seemed relieved to hear that. She smiled. How easily the lie had come to her.

'Well...' she began, but then she sensed a presence near her, very close by, and a fleeting touch of something cool and very slightly moist on the back of her hand. A quick glimpse and there they were, fading and drying already, two bare footprints that seemed to be waiting, hungry for attention.

'You okay?' he said.

'Yes, just tired. Let's find you a room, eh?'

When they were halfway up the stairs, he said, 'You won't get in trouble will you?'

'It's fine,' she said. 'As long as nothing is damaged or whatever... We're not going to have wild parties are we?'

'God, no.'

'Okay, that's my room,' she indicated the closed door opposite the bathroom. 'How about you have this room, next to it?' She led him into the master bedroom. It was a big room, high-ceilinged, twenty-two feet by eighteen, with three tall sash windows, each with the original wooden shutters. There were long yellow brocade curtains that pooled on the floor and were faded in places. The bed with its walnut headboard stood in the centre of the room, the bare mattress was indecently pink and shiny.

Lawrence put his bags on the floor, then unrolled the

sleeping bag and laid it out along one half of the bed. It was one of those high-altitude sleeping bags, a black cocoon that was narrower at the feet than the upper body, like a sarcophagus.

'There's plenty of bedding; pillows, blankets, sheets, eider-downs,' she said.

'This will be fine' he said.

'But…'

It looked so temporary and so out of place, that sleeping bag on the luxurious satin of the mattress. He does not mean to stay, she thought, he can't wait to escape.

He busied himself with his stuff, going through the bags, not unpacking but searching for something. Eventually he came to a limp-looking roll of faded purple towel and a striped nylon wash bag.

'Would it be OK if I had a wash? Need to shave,' he said, rubbing a hand over his bristly chin, so that a faint rasping sound could be heard.

'Yes. Yes, of course. The bathroom's just here. Have a shower.'

He went in and she hovered at the open door.

'We'll have to sort out some money for bills,' he said, as if in answer to her watching him.

'Plenty of time,' she said.

He turned on the shower and held a hand under, testing it, then steam began to gather and rise and he withdrew his hand. Smiling awkwardly, he crossed the room and closed the door in her face.

At college, as the days went by, he behaved towards her exactly as he had always done. He did not sit beside her in lectures, nor share a table in the refectory. They did not walk to college together and after the last lecture of the day he always seemed to be caught up in a laughing conversation with one group of students or another.

To punish him she had not yet given him his own set of keys.

Yet each evening they ate together. She had an allowance, she explained, for expenses, and this covered all the bills, even food. She bought ready meals from Marks and Spencer and heated them in the oven, decanting them onto the best plates and adding flourishes like side salads and steam-in-the-bag vegetables. There was always wine too, though he professed at first not to like it. She put fresh flowers on the table and lit the candles in the silver candelabra.

They started, from desultory beginnings, to have real conversations, though the focus was always weighted towards him, she, having much to hide, used a subtle sleight of hand to keep herself in the shadows.

Only two years before he had been an outstanding athlete; excelling at cricket, rugby, long-distance running, swimming and basketball. Then he'd had his accident while rock climbing.

'But I was lucky,' he said, and she thought it would be luckier not to fall at all, though did not say this. 'I could have been paralysed. I could have been dead. Instead, a year and a half in hospital and I'm as right as rain. Just out of shape. Look!' He pulled his wallet from his back pocket, took out a newspaper clipping. There he was, a god of a man in Speedo swimming trunks, every muscle toned and lean; pecs, biceps, abs, quads. His face, stripped of the plump cheeks and double chin, was that of a Hollywood film star, a young dimpleless Robert Mitchum crossed with Jake Gyllenhaal.

She passed it back to him quickly, afraid to linger over this image.

He'd also revealed more about the quarrel with his father. Lawrence said his dad had left the family when he was too young to remember. Deserted us, was how he put it. The father who had promised to pay his rent, but hadn't and wouldn't answer his calls.

Term broke up for Easter and without saying anything to her, he disappeared for three weeks. She had already bought enough food for the two of them for the coming week and a turkey crown for Easter Sunday, and a chocolate egg each.

In his room the sleeping bag still lay on the bare mattress and there were a few of his things scattered about, but his rucksack was gone. In the weeks before this she had barely noticed the little naked footprints. Perhaps with him there she had been too distracted to notice them. Perhaps he scared them away? Whatever it was, throughout Easter they were back with a vengeance. She saw them in the bathroom, the hall and landing, in the kitchen, bedroom and living room. Very often they were side-by-side next to her own feet and sometimes seemed to disperse her loneliness, at others to distil it, making it far more potent.

The doorbell rang on the last Friday of the holidays at eight o'clock.

She opened the door to find Lawrence on the threshold. He was tanned and seemed to have lost the last of the excess fat. He wore flip-flops, khaki shorts and a white t-shirt.

'Hi,' he said, hefting the rucksack from his back and onto the floor. Not wanting to look at his face, she found herself concentrating on his feet. There were grains of sand still visible between his toes. She hated him for that, for making her remember long ago summer days when she had come home from the beach, sand everywhere and the sea pulsing in her head, the waves still visible when she shut her eyes to sleep.

'Hello,' she said as coldly as she could, but he seemed oblivious.

'Think I'll have a shower,' he said. 'Is there anything to eat?'

She turned sharply on her heel, went to the kitchen and crashed about with pots and pans, browning meat, chopping onions, garlic, mushrooms, chillies.

She heard the creak of the floorboards overhead and the rattle of the pipes as the shower was turned on.

She boiled rice and poured half a bottle of Claret into the sauce. Drank the other half, then opened a second bottle.

The little feet beside her seemed to wobble unsteadily. Her little ghost was drunk, she thought, as she sloshed more wine into a tumbler and drank deeply.

'Smells great!' He was standing in the doorway, his hair still wet, his face gleaming, a pair of loose white linen trousers covering his lower half, while his chest was bare. She turned away quickly, again afraid to let her gaze linger over that taut, muscled skin, the black hair that gathered in the centre of his chest and ran in a line over his flat stomach.

'Can I have a glass?' he asked and when she looked up, she saw that he had put a t-shirt on.

He began to potter about, arranging cutlery on the table in the adjoining room, lighting the candles. Then he put music on; soft swirling pipes and insistent drums, the sound of a night far away in Morocco or Tunisia. Hand claps and a woman's voice, a rhythmic ululating lament.

She slopped the food onto plates, splashes of tomato

everywhere, rice spilled on the stove top, the floor, the counter.

'Can I help?' he asked.

She shook her head, unable to speak. A plate in each hand and the wine bottle tucked under her arm.

'Oops,' he said, coming closer, reaching behind her so that she thought for one moment he was going to put his arms around her. 'You left the gas on.' The pan that had held the rice was blackening and fizzing.

She lurched unsteadily forward and made it through to the dining room without a mishap, tipping the bottle so a little wine sloshed out on to the tablecloth. He filled their glasses and she drained hers immediately. Being this drunk, she thought, is like being in deep water. At the bottom of the ocean with all that weight above you.

'Wow!' he said. 'I've really missed this.'

She half closed one eye in order to focus on him across the table.

'The food?' she said, slurring horribly.

'The food, the house, you and me chilling. Everything.'

By candlelight, even through her drunken haze, he seemed to shine like a Greek god, Apollo or Eros or Dionysus. She tried to shrug, wishing to show him that she couldn't care less if he was there or not. She should just let herself drown she thought, pour more wine down her open throat, let the waves consume her.

Her glass was wet as if a small damp hand had touched it. All around the table, she seemed to see stumbling little footprints as if a child had run around in giddy circles, revelling in this new sensation, this drunkenness.

'So, where did you go?' he asked.

'Huh?'

'Where did you go while they were here?'

'Who-oo?' she said thinking guiltily of the little ghost.

'The owners. You said they'd be back for the holidays.'

Had she said such a thing? Even sober it was hard to keep track of all her lies.

He was watching her face, waiting for an answer.

'They come and go,' she said. 'Like little ghosts.'

He laughed.

'You're funny,' he said. 'I missed that. I missed you.'

This was too much. She rose to her feet, swayed for a second, then walked, her upper body tipping forward perilously, from the room.

Upstairs, she collapsed on her bed fully clothed, then passed out. In the night she drifted in and out of watery dreams and at times awoke to the sounds of rattling pipes and gurgling water. At dawn, with her bladder full and her head throbbing, she tiptoed to the bathroom, relieved herself and drank handfuls of cool, clear water from the tap. The house was silent and still, the door to his room was closed. He had said he missed her, she remembered; that she was funny. He'd laughed and smiled and lit the candles and put on that mysterious and strangely seductive music.

She stood in the hallway gazing towards his room. Should she go in there? Silently climb onto the bed beside him? But there was no soft duvet to lift so that she could snuggle under. He would be in his cocoon of a sleeping bag, the mattress beside him, pink and bare, slippery, cold and unyielding.

In the morning she would make up his bed properly, take away that sleeping bag, put it in the wash or at least turn it inside out and put it on the line to air in the spring sunshine.

She might also confess her lies.

She took a few steps closer to his room, wanting to sense his nearness, to hear his breathing. Then smiling to herself, she returned to her room, undressed, got properly into bed and in seconds she was asleep.

She was awoken by a door banging downstairs and ran to the window in time to see Lawrence jogging down the path towards the gates. She could just make out the thin white wires of an MP3 player trailing from the pocket of his sweatshirt.

She took a long shower, shaving her legs, then applying body lotion. She had neglected herself for too long. She put on a dress she'd found in one of the wardrobes. It was worn soft with age and there was a tear beneath one of the arms, but it was a pretty print and a flattering style.

She made up the bed in the master bedroom and hung his sleeping bag on the line to air. She was in the kitchen waiting for the kettle to boil, when a sudden breeze fluttered at her bare legs, preceding the slammed front door.

'Do you want lunch?' she called.

He came and stood beside her, gently touched her shoulder. 'This is nice. You look pretty in a frock.'

He paused a moment, then kissed her cheek.

'I need a soak,' he said. 'Not used to this much exercise. Won't be long.'

She switched the radio on, turned up the volume and fairly danced about the kitchen, washing lettuce, chopping tomatoes, cucumber, spring onions. She fried mushrooms, leftover potato, onions and ham, then set them to one side, meaning to add the beaten eggs at the last moment.

Everything grew cold in the pan as the minutes went by. She sipped her tea and went to the window, the apple tree was in blossom and the rhubarb was unfurling its giant leaves. His sleeping bag was hanging on the line like a great bat, its wings folded and its head down. Lifeless.

How long had he been upstairs?

Too long, she thought, and her heart seemed to flutter inside her chest, to quiver like an insubstantial jellyfish. She raced up the stairs, the bathroom door was shut and no sound came from behind it. As she looked she saw a trail of watery footsteps stepping from the bathroom and crossing the landing. Each print evaporated as a new one appeared.

★

He did not drown. It had been something to do with his fall from the cliff two years before, a small bleed seeping slowly into his brain that the doctors had missed. There was no water in his lungs, they said, it could have happened at anytime, anywhere, but she – because she had been the caretaker – she knew better.

MECHANICS

Georgina and Charlotte left the field where the circus tent was, and walked to the top of the hill that overlooked it. They went together. They always went together. They had no choice.

They were twins. Or more precisely Siamese twins, joined at the hip (or so the story went). There was no escape. Only this walk together in their artfully constructed twin dresses. Georgina with her right arm around her sister's back. Charlotte, likewise, with her left arm around Georgina's, their legs hidden under their long skirts and petticoats, their waists narrow and tightly corseted, swelling into shapely hips. Each bowed slightly towards the inclined scrub grass as they climbed upwards.

Sometimes one of the girls might slip or stumble on a loose rock or wet grass, but the other would tug her upright, then jostling a little to right themselves, they continued on their way. At the top, if it was dry, they would seat themselves on a grassy hummock and gaze down at the brightly painted tents and vehicles of the circus gathered in a familiar cluster below.

The year was 1932, though the style of dress they habitually wore belonged to an earlier age. This was their mother's idea, and Father, as was his habit, readily agreed.

They were not beautiful, at least not in the conventional sense, but had good figures and clear skin, and long curls of glossy brown hair, which was usually worn with a scarlet ribbon tied in a bow at the crown. It was a hairstyle that their mother herself had worn when she was a girl of thirteen in 1904.

Once the twins were comfortably installed on their grass throne, one took from her pocket a silver case in which a row of thin brown cheroots were imprisoned. She selected two, while her sister fished in her pocket for matches.

Charlotte had the advantage of a free right hand, while Georgina had to either struggle with her left hand, or use her right, but first she had to wriggle to free it from the press of her sister's body which ruined the effect of their unusual appearance. This was how their mother had instructed them to do everyday things; as if they were a single entity with only two arms, but four legs and two heads. They had also been trained to speak as one, saying in perfect chorus, 'Hello, how do you do? I do believe that the weather is improving, don't you think?' In order to make these seemingly spontaneous and simultaneous speeches they had rehearsed multiple variations along with a series of subtle gestures that communicated which phrase should be uttered. It was Georgina who usually took the lead in these transactions with the world, but Charlotte could at times be singular in transmitting different choices that made for bizarre conversation. For example, only days before the leader of the local town council had asked the girls if they enjoyed the rolling hills and lush pastures of that part of Wales, Georgina twirling a finger through a glossy ringlet, signalled that they should say, 'Why, thank you kind sir, everything has pleased us greatly!' But Charlotte had petulantly (as much as sneezing can be petulant) sneezed three times, which was the code for, 'Our dear mother wept bitterly over it and cannot be consoled!'

Georgina sensing the comedy in this answer took a deep breath before they spoke the words in unison together. The council leader was taken aback, 'Is she an invalid?' he asked. To which the girls replied, somewhat mysteriously, 'It is said there are two ways to milk a cow.' The poor man had tried on such a variety of expressions in quick succession in his confusion and grown redder and redder in the face until they thought he might suffer an apoplexy. After that they took their leave with haste as both were stifling a great fit of the giggles.

But now, as each held an aromatic cheroot close to her lips they spoke to one another in a whispered conversation that made it clear that their joined bodies contained two distinct personalities.

'Shall we write to Mother tonight?' Georgina asked.

'Oh, I suppose we ought. Otherwise there'll be hell to pay.'

'And when we go to town, shall we also go to the bank.'

'Oh, yes. Good idea. How much do we have this time?'

Georgina thought about this and then said, 'Almost five pounds.'

'So tonight we'll write, then in the morning?'

'First thing.'

'To the post office.'

'Then the bank.'

The girls' aim was to save enough money to go to America, a plan which their parents would not approve, so much of this business with bank accounts was kept strictly between themselves.

Charlotte took one last long and satisfactory puff on her cheroot, rolling the smoke around and out of her mouth like a cloud of unspoken thoughts, then dropped the remains onto the earth and ground it out with the heel of her black leather boot.

The following day, the sisters walked towards the track on the northern side of the field and followed a rutted path that in turn led to the road into town. They passed an apple orchard with new young apples, gold and green hanging from the branches, and a field whose only occupant was a single brown bull who occasionally took short exploratory runs, his mind full of soft-eyed, soft-flanked cows, or perhaps of the farmer himself tossed high in the air on his horns, then caught – a ruddy-cheeked Welsh matador skewered like a cherry on a cocktail stick.

The sisters spoke excitedly of America and their dreams of going there. They would join Barnum and Bailey's Circus, they'd appear on stage at Dreamland in Coney Island, they'd be the toast of New York City.

They passed along the dusty road by the edge of St Madoc's Church, with its marble headstones and simple wooden crosses, whispering excitedly about Broadway and neon lights and all the handsome swells they'd meet.

So far they had saved up sixteen pounds, two shillings and nine-pence ha'penny. They needed quite a bit more, but they have been living frugally, having made an arrangement with Pedro the Marvellous Four-Legged Boy to (for a share of the food) cook supper for him every evening, then wash the dishes and sweep his caravan floor.

They have been offered very large sums of money to undress for certain men – some of them purporting to be scientists or doctors with a purely professional interest in the sisters' bodies. Others made no pretence of their real purpose and, when rejected, looked at the twins in frank amazement to have their good, hard-earned money turned down – the girls did work for the circus after all, which made them, like actresses and dancers, certain to be prostitutes.

However the sisters have always said no to these proposals to show themselves naked, and the careful styling of their hair, the turn-of-the-century costumes added to their image of old-fashioned modesty.

They were aware of the desire they provoked in certain men; the idea of a double conquest, a two for one body, the unavoidable presence of a voyeur as envious or frightened witness to the deflowering. Yes, that combined with hungry curiosity; the need to investigate whatever fleshy ligaments or muscle joined these two, to see and touch and invent all sorts of erotic possibilities.

The sky was milky with clouds, pale grey and yet also bright. Perhaps it would rain later, or not. The sisters had no shadows.

They walked in silence for a little time, enjoying the sound of the birdsong and the quiet scrape of their feet on the dry earth. Then suddenly, exploding into sound and vision up ahead, a flock of cyclists poured around the twisting road. The cyclists were three, four or even five abreast. Girls with pigtails and scrubbed faces, boys with pomaded hair, faces slick with sweat, most of them in khaki and sand-coloured clothes, baggy shorts and neat shirts with breast pockets and lapels. A beret here. A gay cotton headscarf there. One boy brazen in an undervest. Indecent. His arms from the wrist up, white as milk, his hands and face and neck nut-brown.

The twins responded by moving quickly sideways like a crab. Georgina stumbled into a ditch. Charlotte very nearly followed.

There was a screeching of brakes, a chorus of dringing bells. The boys' voices, deep and resonant, let rip with daring curses, the girl cyclists shrieked with fear. The lead bicyclists somehow escaped unscathed, but in the middle there was a tangle of collision amidst the clouds of agitated dust.

Charlotte helped Georgina onto the path. The cyclists who hadn't fallen, dismounted and propped their bikes against the hedge which bent obligingly, then entered the fray of spinning wheels and grazed knees to separate the people from the machinery.

Charlotte and Georgina were only a few feet away, but crept closer. They wanted to help but their linked bodies were cumbersome and awkward, besides which they are shy amongst these young people – who while they may have noticed that the two women were identical twins, wouldn't have understood quite how remarkable Charlotte and Georgina were.

At the centre of the chaos, one girl with pink skin and straw-coloured hair was lying tangled and slain, her beautiful dimpled knee and round weighty leg calf seemingly pierced and twisted in the spokes of a wheel. A fine trail of bright red blood coiled towards her ankle, then slowly dripped into the dust. Her eyes were closed and her breath came out in shallow gasps through pursed lips.

The twins understood from the rallying cries of the flock that this felled bird was called Edna.

There were moments of horror. One girl was violently sick in the ditch. A tall, very thin, pale-faced boy swayed vertiginously as if he was pretending to be a sapling in a high wind.

But then a miracle. Edna was untangled and swept up in the arms of the tallest, most handsome boy. His jaw was square; his anthracite hair oiled into a warrior's helmet, he wore God's thumbprint on his chin, but the devil had joined his black eyebrows together at the bridge of his perfect nose. He carried Edna over a nearby style and into a field full of frightened sheep which immediately raced in terror to its opposite end.

Everyone, including at the rear (with only the slightest difficulty) Charlotte and Georgina, followed.

Edna was draped across the half-kneeling hero like Bernini's *Pieta*. Her face was an ecstasy of pain or perhaps orgasmic joy at the romantic manhandling she was getting, and in front of so many witnesses too.

'Will she be alright, Gerald?' another girl asked, using the opportunity to kneel down next to him, thigh to bare thigh, as she gazed worriedly at Edna.

'Yes, I should think so,' he said, prompting Edna to open her eyes and stare blinkingly at everyone.

'What happened?' she said, then her gaze happened on the twin sisters, and she smiled in greeting.

The others all looked in the same direction. Eighteen pairs of eyes appraised the sisters. Georgina gave a signal to her sister by pressing the thumb of her right hand onto Charlotte's shoulder. Both sisters took an intake of breath and began to speak, as they have been taught, in unison.

'Hello, we're the Kennedy sisters; we're very pleased to meet you!'

They delighted in the astonished looks they received from the gathered crowd.

The handsome boy stepped forward and offered his hand. Charlotte shook it with her right, and then more awkwardly Georgina shook with her left.

'Pleased to meet you!' the young man said. 'I'm Gerald

Davies, and this,' he swept his arm in a broad circle indicating the other cyclists, 'is the Cwm Bach Cycling and Rambling Club.'

The club members all offered a greeting, some saying 'hello' or 'good morning,' others just waving or smiling.

There was something terribly wholesome about the young people, they exuded fresh air and energy and freedom. The twins felt the pinch of envy as they appraised the young ladies in particular with their comfy shorts or culottes, their muscular legs and no-nonsense hairstyles and shoes. The company of such handsome young men was not to be overlooked either, especially this one, Gerald; he would certainly be a catch.

After a lot of debate among the group it was decided that in order for Edna and some of the others to rest and recover, they would have their morning tea break immediately and, like ants each certain of their particular purpose, the group set about making a fire, boiling water and swilling out a huge enamel tea pot and many tin mugs.

Edna begged the twins to join them and the twins, without a nudge or pinch or cough of consultation agreed.

As luck would have it, here near the edge of the field was a felled tree that the farmer had not yet cleared, and the sisters sat on it. They were watched. They knew that they were being scrutinised, but subtly, politely, with warm smiles and eyes that do their interrogative work askance.

Gerald brought them their mugs of tea and Edna offered them buttered scones, which she said, with a smiling gaze that flickered mostly in Gerald's direction, she had baked herself last night.

The club members arranged themselves in a loose circle around the twins, and chattered amongst themselves, giggling and exchanging silly banter.

The sky began to clear and grow bluer. It would not rain today after all.

'We had an awful fright back there,' said Edna who was sitting near Gerald and breaking off bite-sized chunks from her scone before eating them.

'Oh yes, but you're alright aren't you, Edie?'

Edna touched her bandaged knee, in the centre of the white cloth a pink stain the size of a penny was beginning to show. 'Yes,' she said, 'I suppose so.'

'You see, she's awfully brave, not like a girl at all,' Gerald said.

Edna looked uncertain at this. Being brave was good, but not being like a girl wasn't so good. Edna looked at the twins carefully, they were so strange, like china figurines with their long skirts and old-fashioned hair and tiny waists. Edna was used to identical twins as her cousins were also twins, but Betty and Joan were never like this, so strange and secretive.

Gerald said, 'You two are very close, aren't you? I suppose that's because you're twins?'

Charlotte ran her fingers in a drumming wave on Georgina's shoulder near the neck. Both spoke, 'Yes we're twins, but not like ordinary twins – we're Siamese.'

'Good lord,' said Gerald, 'like Chang and Eng, the original Siamese twins? How fascinating.'

The girls nodded in perfect unison.

'Oh how awful,' said Edna, 'do you mean that you're joined together? How sad.'

The twins were silent.

'Well, I don't see that it's all that sad,' offered Gerald.

'Oh it is,' said Edna, 'it's awfully, awfully sad. I mean you can't ever ride a bike or go for a swim. Or…' She stopped then and, blushing, lowered her head.

The girls didn't answer.

'And you can't ever, ever get married can you? Not either of you and that's the saddest thing ever!' Edna said in a rush of passion and worked herself up until she looked ready to burst into tears.

Gerald looked at Edna, then at the twins. He suddenly grew flustered. He was imagining the mechanics of marriage. The sex act. He'd done it already, lots of times, with Mrs Dundridge whose husband had died in the war, and who lived down the road from him. Gerald's mother had persuaded him to help Mrs Dundridge with odd jobs for a bit of pocket money; carrying coal up from the cellar, digging in the garden, moving furniture. Mrs Dundridge was lonely and still young, just 27 when he first went. He'd been fifteen. She'd said that with all his skills in the garden and the carpentry and so on he'd make a perfect husband one day. Then lowering her voice she'd added that there were other things a man should know. *Mechanics.* And she hadn't meant Meccano.

Gerald couldn't stop imagining those two strange sisters naked. Himself naked too, and those two female bodies closing in on him like wings, or like a hinged mirror, two identical faces swooping closer, and legs and arms entangling him, hands everywhere.

He was getting far too excited thinking about this, and so he took it out on Edna.

'I think you're being a bit rude, Edie. I mean, gosh, it isn't our business, you know,' he said primly.

Edna blushed. 'I'm sorry,' she said, then broke off another piece of scone, but did not eat it. Instead she threw it towards some sparrows and starlings that had settled hopefully just beyond the group.

The twins whispered to one another, taking it in turn to cup the other's ear as they spoke. They made the decision to break with the pre-rehearsed speeches, and speak as individuals.

'It's alright,' said Charlotte, 'we know it's strange for you, but we've been like this all our lives.'

Edna brightened. 'Yes, I suppose you must be used to it. People saying the wrong thing, I mean.'

'People can be very cruel,' Georgina said, 'but they don't always mean it. And others are very kind too.' Georgina didn't like Edna one bit and wished she'd go away. Charlotte felt the same. Both sisters wished Edna would go away. Silly Edna with her crocodile tears and pity.

They finished their tea.

'Well,' said Charlotte, 'time to get on or we won't be back in time for the show.'

'The show?' said Gerald.

'Will you escort us over the stile?' asked Georgina, careful to hold only Gerald in her gaze.

'Bye-bye,' the girls called.

The members of the club chorused their goodbyes in response.

Gerald walked by the side of Charlotte. When they were out of earshot, he asked again, 'What show?'

'Oh, the circus,' said Georgina. 'You'll see it a bit further down the road; there's a painted banner with our picture on it.'

'Why don't you come and see us,' Charlotte said. 'We'd like to see you.'

She was careful to emphasise 'you' making the word rock

44

with significance.

Gerald pictured the enfolding wings of their two bodies again.

'Well,' he said, 'that's awfully nice. I think I'd like that.'

He watched them on their way down the lane, noticed how their arms encircled one another's waists, how their feet worked in perfect union.

'Oh, what a pity,' said Edna when he rejoined the group. 'Weren't they just awfully sad?'

'Oh, yes,' he said, 'I suppose so.'

'Can you help me up, Gerald,' said Edna and she made the pretence of a painful struggle, held her hands up to be eased to her feet, to be saved.

Gerald hardly noticed Edna's outstretched arms; above him in the trees he heard the sudden beating of wings. He turned at the sound but there was nothing he could see, only the quickening of his heart, which pulsed and fluttered like a trapped and dying bird.

THE MURDER STONE

Most dreadful MURDER!
Here on the night of June 1st
in the year of our Lord 1787
did Matilda Jones wrongfully and
most cruelly smite down
Eliza Jones, her crippled sister.

'That's my birthday – give or take 200 years.'

'Your name too,' he said flatly.

'Oh, yeah. I…' she began, but he had walked away striding along the path to Moel Lâs. She read the text again or at least the part of it that wasn't hidden by a thick clot of weeds.

She turned and saw he had already put a good 200 yards or so between them. Another glance at the stone and she was running to catch up with him.

They walked in silence for the most part, each lost in his or her thoughts. The path rose steadily passing over straw-coloured hills and plateaux under a great blue sky. Here and there it followed a tumbling stream that sparkled and gurgled. Flocks of sheep stood on higher ground eyeing them warily, or scattering in a panic, one following another, many of them swinging great pregnant bellies that broadened their already wool-swollen girths, their little legs like brittle, improbable sticks. Occasionally other walkers passed, exchanging a greeting or a comment on the fine weather after so many months of rain.

In the distance Moel Lâs hunched its giant's shoulder, darker than the surrounding land and reminding her of Yeats' Ben Bulben in Sligo.

When they reached the lake they stopped to read the information board, but she hardly took it in, she was still thinking about the murder stone.

'Drink some water,' he said, and for an instant she imagined he meant the expanse of water before them, but he was putting his bottle to his mouth and tipping back his head. She did the same.

'You okay?' he asked, looking at her carefully.

'Yep, fine.'

He had been told about her illness then; no doubt Iain had thoroughly briefed him. Perhaps, she thought, perhaps this date was undertaken as a kindness and was not driven by a real desire to get to know her, to court her.

Court – an old-fashioned word for an old-fashioned date. A drive, then a walk and picnic. He probably already had a girlfriend. She would have been told that he was taking Iain's sister out.

'Poor thing,' the girlfriend would have said. 'Be nice to her won't you.'

The path followed a high ridge that loomed over the lake. Distant figures, groups of three, of two, of five, moved minutely along it silhouetted against the sky.

He was tall and extraordinarily good looking. Like Iain he was studying medicine at Kings. Unlike Iain he came from money.

They toiled upward, still hardly speaking, she might have made more of an effort at conversation, but what was the point? There was nothing to be invested in this. The further they walked the more she was certain that, really, they were going nowhere.

'What about here?' he said, stopping and unhitching the rucksack from his shoulders. She made to sit down, but he stopped her. A picnic blanket was produced, Black Watch tartan, backed with a waterproof sheet. She sat and he produced a thermos, then package after package of food. A salad of raw grated vegetables, another of brown rice, sunflower seeds and tahini. Nut rissoles. A weighty brick of homemade wholemeal bread.

She ate but without enthusiasm or pleasure. Without much concern either, what did it matter if some of the spinach stuck in her teeth?

Her mind turned again to the murder stone. Her instinct had been to clear the weeds away and read the entire text. She would have copied it in her notebook, made a rough sketch of it, noted the exact place. She would have done that even without the coincidence of the date and the name. With them her interest was even stronger. She resolved to return, next time alone.

'Had enough?' he said.

Everything was carefully packed away again and they set off, her following him and wishing she could do something to attract him to her, to see her as more than Iain's troubled and sickly sister. She wished she could think of something funny or clever to say.

If she married him this was how it would be, everything wholesome and healthy, nothing dark and dirty and dangerous. Sex, she thought, would be akin to a gynaecological examination and a work-out in the gym. This thought made her laugh out loud.

'Something funny?' he said, frowning as he turned to look at her.

'Nothing.'

'Do you always laugh at nothing?' He made it sound like an interrogation; recognition of a symptom.

'There's nothing wrong with me you know.'

'I never said there was.'

'Good.'

'Look. We seem to have got off on the wrong foot. It's me. Never know what to say.'

'Well, let's just walk then.'

'Ok,' he says.

Along the high ridge they go. Down by the lake another couple are standing where they'd stood by the information board and yet another man and woman are heading away from the lake, their hands clasped and swinging like children. She might be seeing the past. Or the future.

'That gravestone back there,' she says.

'It's a murder stone.'

'Oh. Isn't that the same thing?'

'No. It's a memorial rather than a grave. Unconsecrated ground.'

'Oh.'

'I didn't think it would interest you.'

'Why not?'

'Girls don't like that sort of thing.'

'I thought it was interesting.'

'Because of the name.'

'And the date.'

'A spooky coincidence?' He altered his voice slowing and deepening it, intoning, 'And two hundred years later her direct descendant, Matty was born…'

'Do you know how many Joneses there are in Wales?'

'You might be though.'

'Who would want to be related to a murderer?'

'Hey, calm down. I was only kidding.'

Why is she so angry? Like a creature who has been cornered and is lashing out? Even if the 'date' is in reality only a kindness, he doesn't deserve this.

'Look,' she says and he does just that, looks at her face and obediently awaits her next words. She shakes her head. What is the point?

There is a silence, then he says, 'Come on.'

They set off again, walk to the end of the ridge, then take the path that drops down behind it, so that the lake can no longer be seen. The landscape changes, they go into a wood, the bluebells aren't in flower yet but the ground is covered with clumps of their dark broad leaves.

'We should come back in a couple of weeks,' he says.

'Come back?' She is surprised; could it be that he really wants to spend time with her?

'Well, if you'd like.'

Would she like? Would she like what? More medicine? More well-meaning gestures?

'Why?' she asks bluntly.

'Because of the bluebells.' He is unsettled now.

She stops walking. 'You don't have to do this.'

'Do what?'

'Be kind to me. Do Iain a favour; take his crazy sick sister out.'

His mouth, his handsome mouth drops open in surprise. His eyes widen.

She looks away.

'Is that what you think? That I asked you out because

Iain wanted me to?'

She still doesn't meet his eye. Of course he would deny it. Deny it until death and doomsday. She shrugs and walks on.

'Matty!'

She hears him just behind her. The path is narrow, looping up and down through trees, over rocks. Now the river is visible far below, deep and rushing, rain-filled, dirty yellow looking in places.

She wishes he weren't behind her, she senses his eyes on her, seeing when she stumbles or struggles. Poor cripple girl.

And then they are out of the woods and back at the car park. Still in awkward silence they go to the car. He opens the hatchback, takes off his muddy boots and puts shoes on. She looks down at her own feet, thick mud cakes the soles like the rubber bumpers around dodgem cars and she has no clean shoes to put on. She begins to wipe them on a clump of grass.

'It's ok,' he says. 'It doesn't matter.'

'It does. I'll make your car dirty.'

'Take them off then.' He guides her to the car, makes her sit on the tailgate, bends and begins to unlace her boots. He puts them next to his own, small replicas of his, brown leather, the same style and make. She hadn't noticed that until now. She was about to remark on the coincidence, but she's shocked into silence as he has lifted her up. One arm around her back, the other under her knees. He carries her to the passenger door, manages somehow to open it.

'Have you read Tess of the d'Urbervilles?' he says, putting her gently into the seat.

'No.'

51

He closes the door and goes round to his side.

'Why?'

He puts the key in the ignition. 'I'll buy you a copy.'

She frowns a question at him.

'If you read it you'll know I really don't care about a bit of mud in my car.'

After that she avoids him. He rings several times and texts her. One text simply said, 'Bluebells?' She refuses to discuss it with Iain. Eight years go by, then she is at a friend's house and they watch the film *Tess*. The earnest young man, Angel Clare, carries the girls one by one across the flooded lane. Tess is last. He has carried each of the others only to have a chance to lift her in his arms. To press her close to him, to feel her weight in his arms, to sense her warmth, her scent.

She begins to sob.

'I know,' her friend says.

'No, you don't know. You really don't.'

More years pass and in an idle hour, she looks up murder stones on her laptop. Quickly she finds 'her' stone and the full text is revealed. 'Matilda Jones was hung at Carmarthen for her crime protesting her innocence to the last. On his deathbed in the year of 1831, Eliza's husband Thomas Williams confessed to the crime and begged forgiveness for the destruction of two blameless women.'

Now we have gone full circle she thought, but knew in her heart that she had taken her own path and it had been the wrong one.

A BIRD BECOMES A STONE

The film Sarah had volunteered to act in was written and directed by a Welsh girl called Catrin, who was at college in Bristol. She'd brought a crew of other students to Wales, one to do sound, another was a cameraman. There was also a sulky girl with bad skin called Morgana whose role was not explained. They drove in a grubby white VW van up to the Brecon Beacons, careering and bumping along narrow tracks in search of good locations. The cameraman drove and the girl with bad skin sat up front because she claimed she'd get carsick otherwise. So the other three had to suffer in the back, wedged in among the film equipment and two plastic sacks of what seemed to be dirty laundry but turned out to be props and costume.

Sarah played the main role. According to the storyboard a lot of footage would consist of her running through woods, along a shoreline (brooding clouds and crashing waves in the background) and along treacherous mountain paths. The schedule demanded that they shoot with her for three days, then on the fourth and fifth days another actor would join them. He was to play a man who had molested her as a child. The chief premise of the film was that every impression in the early sequences led the audience to believe she was being chased, but actually it emerged that her character was the pursuer. The hunted becomes the hunter.

They parked at a lay-by above a stream. The day was still

and unusually warm, white puffs of cumulus clouds moved lazily across a yawning blue sky.

'This weather is crap,' Catrin said.

The girl with the bad skin sat on a rock and stared hatefully at the rest of them as they unloaded the van.

From eleven o'clock until almost two, Sarah helped Catrin and the sound man scatter torn white sheets along the side of the stream while the cameraman shouted directions at them. At two they stopped for a lunch made by Catrin's mother. Sandwiches with cheap white bread, some sort of meat that might have been pork or possibly turkey, hard-boiled eggs, crisps and an assortment of chocolate-covered biscuits which were warm and sticky and reminded her too much of long journeys in the back of her parents' car; of her loneliness as an only child.

After lunch Sarah climbed into the back of the van and struggled into the costume they had brought for her; a grubby, ivory-coloured floor-length dress. It had a plunging front and tied behind her neck leaving her back bare. It was made of artificial satin and the rough skin on her hands caught on it like tiny barbs.

In this scene she was meant to wander along by the stream charting a course between one discarded rag and another. Catrin showed Sarah some photographs taken after a battle; women searching for their menfolk in a field littered with the corpses of soldiers, explaining that this was the atmosphere she wanted to convey.

Sarah set off barefoot; in places mud oozed between her toes. The dress was thin, she shivered as the sun began to drop behind the mountains, but she persevered.

That night Sarah dreamt that she was filming the scene over and over, but her dream was invaded by the war photograph and as she stared at each flung-down rag, the torn scraps came to life turning into dreadful ghosts with scarred and half-flayed skin who moaned and tried to touch her.

The next day Catrin was overjoyed as weighty blue-grey cumulonimbus began to gather behind the mountains threatening an approaching storm.

'We're going further north today, then as far as Dolgellau on Thursday.'

There was little time wasted on the second day; they parked on a bleak mountain with a ribbon-like road running through it. Plynlimon hunkered under dark skies to the north.

'Now just run towards the camera but look beyond it, not directly at it.'

She ran. Barefoot in wet grass peppered with shiny black sheep droppings, her long dress saturated up to her thighs. A few times she fell but pulled herself up and stumbled on.

'That was brilliant! It looks so real when you fall,' Catrin said.

'Hey,' the sound guy said, touching her arm gently. 'Is that blood? Did you hurt yourself?'

She looked down; the dress was torn over her right knee, bright crimson blood mixed with muddy grey stains. She lifted her dress, her knee was grazed and in one place a small cut sent a trickle of red coursing down her leg and over the arch of her foot.

'It's fine,' she said.

The girl with bad skin, Morgana, wrote something in a notebook, then lit a cigarette and wandered off.

Sarah asked the sound guy what Morgana did.

'We *have* to work in teams of four,' he said. 'We're stuck

with Morgana, she's stuck with us. And she hates Catrin and says the film is a pile of romantic twaddle.'

Sarah almost wished she didn't understand the relationship between the four students. She felt angry on behalf of Catrin. To be forced to drag along the dead weight of Morgana just because the college dictated it! The lecturer's reasoning, or so she understood, was that in the real world you had to work with people you didn't get along with, but hell, in the real world Morgana would have been sacked on day one.

Because of this Sarah developed a deeply emotional sense of commitment – she, at least, would do everything in her power to make the film a success, regardless of grazed knees and damp unpleasant conditions.

On the third day, they drove for almost four hours. Sarah had ended up sitting on the floor behind the passenger seat, which was fine until Morgana decided to brush her hair. Morgana's hair was dry and wiry at the ends, greasy at the scalp. The spiky plastic hairbrush made crackling noises as she pulled it through the tangle. Sarah looked up at the sound and noticed how Morgana's hair was plastered to her scalp and wet-looking with grease. She could smell a strong animal odour, pelt and sweat. Stray strands of Morgana's hair were drifting down, landing on Sarah's bare arms, her chest and legs.

'Hey! Do you have to do that?'

Morgana carried on dragging the brush through her hair.

Sarah poked Morgana's shoulder.

'Ow!' said Morgana and craned her head around to look at Sarah.

'Do you have to? You're covering me with hair! It's bloody revolting.'

Morgana pulled a sneering face. 'It's only *hair*.' Then she continued brushing, even more vigorously than before.

'Hey!'

'Get a fucking life!' Morgana said without turning around.

Catrin pulled the van into a lane, and parked halfway up a verge opposite an aluminium cattle gate. Sarah, Justin and Si began to unload the equipment. Morgana sat in the passenger seat with her feet on the dashboard, smoking.

In the distance was a small whitewashed cottage surrounded by a fence made of upright slabs of slender black stone that reminded Sarah of tombstones.

Catrin climbed a stile into the upward-slanted field that led to the house. Si, Justin and Sarah began to pass cases of equipment over the stile. Sarah glanced back to look at Morgana, but a bright shaft of sunlight had caught the windshield turning it into a dazzling mirror so she could not see her.

Rather than go back to the van to change, Sarah hunkered down out of sight by a bent wind-stunted tree to slither out of her jeans, t-shirt and bra, and into her costume. The dress was damp, muddy and bloodstained from the day before. As Sarah stood up, twisting and tugging at the dress so it hung properly, she thought she saw a figure move behind a window in the cottage.

She walked briskly over to where Catrin was. Si had set the camera on a tripod and Catrin was looking through the lens while he stood to one side.

'Catrin,' Sarah said, 'do you think we need permission to film here? I mean it's private property, isn't it?'

'Oh, it'll be fine. Come on, it'll only take twenty minutes or so. Could you go to the furthest end of the fence and just stand there, then look at the house and maybe touch the fence like this?' She demonstrated with a tentative stroke of her fingers in the air.

Sarah took up her position and stood still until Catrin gave the signal. She looked longingly at the house then reached out and tenderly touched the fence, then she noticed Morgana stalking through the field towards her, her expression midway between deadpan and a scowl. Sarah heard the tinny sound of some awful dance music coming closer. Morgana was carrying a boom box in one hand and a tartan rug in the other. She flung herself down on the grass about seven feet from where Sarah stood.

Moments before the air had been filled with birdsong and the occasional murmur of wind; now Techno was renting the air with its jagged infernal beats, thudding and stuttering at high speed.

Sarah, without looking at Morgana, ran over to the crew.

'Aren't you going to stop her?' Sarah asked breathlessly as she drew near.

'Oh, it's okay, she's out of shot,' Catrin said.

'Yeah, it's fine,' said Si, looking up from the viewfinder. 'I've just got you, the fence, the mountains. Looking good.'

'And the sound?'

'Oh, it's not a problem,' Catrin said. 'Some bits will have music anyway. It'll be fine in the edit.'

'I'm trying to *act* here. To create a mood and an atmosphere. I have to believe it. How the hell can I do it with that bloody noise?'

'Oh,' Catrin bit her lip and looked doubtfully over at Morgana, frowning.

'I think we got it,' Si said. 'First take was good.'

'Okay then, problem solved. It's a wrap. Lunch?'

The next morning Sarah's legs were battered and scabby, some bruises were still purple, others were already yellow as if she'd sponged iodine over them. She had just enough time to eat a yoghurt and drink a strong coffee before she heard the van beeping outside. Justin was sitting in the front seat and seeing Sarah's look of happy surprise at Morgana's absence, said, 'We're meeting up with Morgana tomorrow.' He gave a snorting laugh and rolled his eyes. 'Think we can manage without her?'

Sarah put on the ivory gown once again, noting as she did that it was beginning to smell a little. Sweat and mud and blood; unpleasant but she savoured the scent, breathing it in and assuming the persona of her nameless character.

Catrin and Si set up the camera and were comparing whatever they saw through the lens with a postcard of the painting 'Christina's World'. As she drew near, Sarah overheard them talking about the fact there was not the slightest breeze.

The day was overcast; opalescent pale grey clouds hung overhead holding the world in silence and stillness.

'Can you kind of crawl through the grass, about here?' Catrin had set off up the hill until she was fifteen feet away. 'Like this,' Catrin got down with her back to the camera and lay with her body twisted at the waist and groped in the direction of the ruined cottage.

Sarah copied her and Catrin ran back and forth a few times to make minute adjustments.

'Now, if you could keep absolutely still. We're gonna run the camera for a while and out of shot I'm going to flap a board so hopefully your hair will lift and move in the wind.'

Sarah held the pose. She was aware of a waft of air passing over her, but didn't know if they were getting the effect they wanted. The pose was awkward, her weight unnaturally distributed, within a minute or so her right shoulder began to quiver in protest.

They hadn't told her much about her character, so she made up her own scenario. It was in that house that she'd grown up. Her mother had died or left. She had suffered. Then one day she had run away. Now she was back, but somehow she was unable to move from this spot. The memories were too much. She could neither go forward nor back. There was no future and no past, only this empty field, this broken-down house and the wind gently rippling her hair.

'Brilliant! Cut.'

Si dismantled the camera and followed the two women back to the van. Sarah wrapped herself in a blanket that smelled of engine oil and wet dog and ate a scotch egg without complaint. She was still in character; she let it wash over her, this sadness, this beaten-dog attitude, this sense of loss.

They did more scenes, Catrin and Si and Justin worked almost silently together, each seeming to know instinctively what was required of them. The absence of Morgana was almost as palpable as her presence.

The atmosphere during the journey home was giddy, as wild and silly as a children's party. They played a game in which each of them sang show tunes and the others had to guess the musical. Then they sang as many songs as they could remember, gleefully at the top of their lungs. 'Bohemian Rhapsody' which Si knew the words to, while the others da-dummed between the bits they knew. Nodding heads in unison, in knowing and ironic parody of *Wayne's World*.

Scaramouch, Scaramouch, can you do the fandango!

Every day of filming should have been like this, would have been if it hadn't been for Morgana.

Ding dong the witch is dead sang Justin as if he'd read Sarah's mind.

That night Sarah fell into bed exhausted, phrases from a dozen songs mingling in a mad melody that trilled in her head. She set her alarm for five a.m. She had almost entirely forgotten Morgana, her ugly face and bad, pock-marked skin, her nasty greasy hair, the animal smell of her.

'I watched the rushes last night,' Catrin said the next day. 'I'm really pleased with it, you've all done a brilliant job, especially you, Sarah.'

Outside the sun shone brightly, though to the north, blue-black clouds were gathering.

Sarah wondered why they tolerated Morgana. She grew more determined that Catrin's film be a success and that in itself was like putting a foot upon the serpent, Morgana's, throat.

The weather worsened as they neared Blaenau Ffestiniog. The mountains loomed, black and implacable, with silvery slivers of waterfalls here and there, and black lakes, and white specks of improbable sheep.

Catrin parked on the verge of a broad lane, one part of which was bordered by high hedges and led into a wood while the other led to a farmhouse that clung to the hillside some way off.

'There they are!' Catrin said, and Sarah saw Morgana and a tall man, the other actor, ambling down the track from the farmhouse.

'You guys start unloading, I'll be back now,' Catrin said, then she got out of the van and jogged up the path to meet Morgana and the stranger.

After twenty minutes or so, Morgana and the man turned around and went off in the direction they had come.

'Okay,' Catrin said breathlessly, 'Sarah, costume. Justin, Si? Can I have a minute?'

Sarah slithered into the bedraggled dress for the last time. It was as if she were donning the shed skin of her character, assuming the mantle of a woman unlike her real self; a wilder creature, a victim, but also one capable, when cornered, of terrible brutality and rage. She pictured her bare foot on the neck of her vanquished enemy once more.

Where had that image come from? It was Old Testament. Vengeance is mine. An eye for an eye. The old fire and brimstone preachers rising up from their barren tombs, shaking their fists at the Sodom and Gomorrah cities of the twenty-first century.

A stone that becomes a bird.

A bird that becomes a flame.

She let the ideas and images flow around her. Snippets and scraps of scenes from films and books and things from her childhood and dreams. Opening the doors to them, instead of slamming them shut with logic.

She shivered, closed her eyes for a moment, hugging herself.

The last day.

Catrin led Sarah and the two young men up the lane into the forest, all of them carrying pieces of equipment. Sarah with a blanket over her and trainers on her bare feet. How strange they must have looked; three young anthropologists leading their captured feral woman back into the woods.

They left the path and entered the pine forest. The trees

were regularly spaced and hardly anything grew underneath, giving it a sort of harsh beauty quite alien from the natural deciduous forests of oak and elm, with moss and bluebells and mushrooms underfoot.

In a clearing under a high ridge Catrin stopped and put down the camera. 'Okay, Sarah, can you stand behind that tree there. We'll begin filming when I shout action but I'd like you to count up to 60 seconds then slowly come out from behind the tree; look around until you're looking up there, turn around a few times, then walk away from the camera. We've got a long view of the woods and I want the figure to keep going and keep going until you're only a tiny speck.'

Sarah nodded. No words now. Sarah was gone. There was no Catrin, no film crew. Just this creature with no name.

By the tree Sarah shed her shoes and the warm blanket. Goosebumps rose up instantly and her nipples hardened in protest. She heard, ACTION! Closed her eyes and counted; one Mississippi, two Mississippi, three Mississippi and when she got to sixty she slowly, gracefully, moved from behind the tree.

She was in the moment. Lost in the zone. She did not think about the camera trained on her, or on three sets of eyes studying her, urging her on.

She gazed about her, looked north, south, east, west, then over at the spot above and beyond the camera. She did not want to catch a glimpse of the camera crew as she did this, but she was genuinely surprised to note that she could not see them. It was as if they had evaporated.

Turning, turning, in her bare feet, like a clockwork toy as its mechanism winds down. Underfoot, earth and pine needles. Ants and beetles. The scurrying highway of minute life. Under stones, spiders and woodlice. Underground, worms and twisted roots and moles.

Then her back was to the camera again and she began the journey forward, away. Off in a straight line into the forest. Off until she could no longer be seen.

She walked slowly, concentrating mainly on staying in a straight line which, given the trees and fallen branches, was harder than she might have imagined.

The part of the forest Catrin had selected for this scene was perfect and afforded Sarah the longest distance to go in one direction without a slope or a natural outcrop to hide her from view.

So she walked, sometimes imagining her figure shrinking in the distance as she did so. The choice of the ivory satin gown was perfect, nothing else, except perhaps a vibrant buzzy scarlet would show up so well against the dark browns and greens of the trees.

At one point she recognised the flaw in this plan, how should she know when she had walked far enough?

Oh, she would know.

Besides which, walking at this preternaturally slow pace and in such an alien and yet repetitive landscape disturbed her judgement of time and space. How long or how far she had gone was in some ways merely a tautological riddle, her job was to walk until she disappeared.

Another minute. Another few steps.

The more we invest in something, the more we have to lose if our nerve fails us.

So Sarah continued on until she at last came to a dry stone wall, beyond which was a scrubby pasture. The edge of the forest.

She turned around and looked back the way she had

come. The trees presented their same featureless regularity; there was no sign of life at their furthest reaches.

The pasture curved down to a copse of deciduous trees, near which twenty or thirty sheep pressed themselves together until, as she watched, one broke away and ran in that panicky silly sheep way, back up the hill, followed very swiftly by the others.

She sighed.

All she had to do was walk back the way she'd come.

The sun came out momentarily warming her skin. Her pace was more normal and after only ten minutes or so she saw the break in the trees and the glint of light upon a camera lens. She picked up her pace in anticipation of their pleasure at her performance; of smiles and hot tea from the flask and the rough warmth of the blanket around her shoulders.

She drew nearer still and saw them more clearly, Catrin standing with her hands on her hips, Justin holding the boom aloft, Si behind the camera. Just as they had been when she had set off. She hadn't expected that, she thought they would have stopped filming by now and would be relaxing, eating their lunch or dismantling the equipment.

No one waved at her or even seemed to register her presence. A change of plan perhaps? As Catrin had been unclear as to where the film was going they may have decided upon this – to record her return just as they had filmed her walking away.

So I shouldn't signal them, Sarah thought, I should just walk on as I have been, show no sign that I have even seen them.

She was perhaps forty yards away when she noticed a fourth figure join the group, the great halo of fuzzy dark hair told her immediately that it was Morgana. She walked behind Si and checked the monitor then nodded, raised her hand and pointed with one finger as if it were a gun in Sarah's direction.

It seemed like some sort of threat. A childish playground sign. Bang-bang, you're dead.

Sarah continued toward them concentrating her gaze to a place just above and beyond the camera, half daydreaming of how she could walk straight up to Morgana and, without a word, slap her ugly face.

She sensed movement near her, but did not turn to see what it was. A small animal or bird perhaps.

She has learned not to be distracted. Once on stage, playing Ophelia in a youth theatre production, swathed in trailing ivy and plastic flowers – *There's fennel for you and columbines* – someone in the front row had a seizure, metal chairs clattered and crashed, but Sarah went on – *There's rue for you, and here's some for me.* Her voice was shaky and broken but unstoppable, because she was, as ever, hopeful.

So now this sudden noise, followed by another is ignored by Sarah, until suddenly there is something, someone standing directly on the path in front of her five or six feet away.

A man. Tall, dressed in black, a heavy coarse overcoat, black trousers, black shoes, a white cotton shirt closed up to the collar, with no tie. A chin that's stained blue-black red with stubble and shaving rash. Lips narrow and pale drawn in a fleshless line. Black eyes in shadowed pits. Cheeks hollow under sharp bones, gaunt and unforgiving.

Sarah makes to go around him. He sidesteps to block her way.

She tries again, this time he raises each of his arms as if in anticipation of catching her.

'Sarah,' he said in a low whisper.

Her own name had never held such terror before. She spun out of reach so that all his hand caught was the trailing sash of the halter neck dress. She felt the bow at her nape unravelling swiftly and silkily, let out a scream and shot a hand up to stop the dress from falling.

'Sarah!' he said again.

She ducked underneath his grasping arms and turned sharply to her left and began to run down the steeply inclined hill. She ran wildly, tripped in places; picked herself up, fell again.

Cut, scratched, ripped, battered, dirtied, swiped by the low branches of spiteful scrubs, bruised by sudden protruding rocks. She came to a level piece of land where the trees were thinner, the undergrowth denser and her running was more controlled. Beyond one set of low bushes, at what looked like the end of the tall pines, she saw a patch of unbroken sky. She raced for it; kicked through, thrashing her arms against the knot of vegetation, gritting her teeth, snarling with the effort then, triumph! She breaks through, pops out of the twisted tangle like a newborn. Out into nothing but air with no hands to catch her, and she is flying, falling, legs and arms comically pedalling as she goes.

Her finest hour.

And no stunt double, not even a straw-filled sack with a dummy's bewigged head to crack on the river rocks below.

'Stupid bloody bitch,' said Morgana, staring down the steep hill in the direction Sarah had fled. 'I knew she'd ruin every-thing, the stupid cow!'

She signalled to the film crew with a hand slicing at her throat. *Cut.*

67

Then turned to the other actor, noticing with disdain the powdery black shadows painted around his eyes.

'Romantic rubbish,' she muttered under her breath. 'Stupid bloody bullshit.'

Catrin caught up with them.

'Where's Sarah?'

Morgana shrugged.

'Was that what you wanted?' the man asked.

'Kind of,' said Catrin.

Then she looked off in the direction Sarah had run. 'Sarah?' she called. Then louder, her hands cupped around her mouth to project her voice further.

'Sa-rah!'

No answer came. Catrin sat down on the carpet of pine needles that covered the hillside. She sighed deeply. Images floated in her mind's eye; the running woman, the woman searching amongst the scattered rags, the one of her sprawled at the bottom of the meadow with the ruined cottage in the distance. The perfect stillness of everything except for a few windblown strands of hair.

All of it better than she could have hoped for. And completed now by this absence. This beautiful haunting question mark.

PRAYER, 1969

A school is not a church, she thought as she pushed open the doors to the entrance foyer with its high ceiling and promise of echoes. One is pure. The other is... She could not quite finish her train of thought. It was jagged, full of barbs and snares that trailed in a filthy stream. Concentrate, she told herself, rise above it. Pray.

The doors to the assembly hall were on her right, to her left was the long corridor lined with the classrooms on the first floor. Ahead of her was the staircase leading up to more classrooms and the door leading to the staff area and offices. The latter she always imagined as a sort of archipelago of rationality and order. The headmaster's office was here, as was the deputy headmistress's, and the supply office and Gestetner machine, as well as the staff common room; smoke-filled from morning to night.

She breathed in deeply; the air here smelt good, cleansed of the accumulating odours of the previous day; the mince and onion smell of the school dinners, or on other days the heavy, clinging scent of fish and frying fat, the chlorine from the swimming pool, the stink of malodorous feet and armpits and groins from the changing rooms, the sharp purple chemical smell that wafted from the duplication machine. And each pupil's individual scent too, cheap perfume, or Pears soap, pine or apple shampoo, or Brylcreem or mint toothpaste, or more rarely those heady and unmistakable smells which came from the effluvia of young bodies; menstrual blood, vomit, sweat, urine, shit, semen.

A part of her wanted to turn around and head back through the glass doors, across the car park, past the iron gates, on down through street after street of identical council houses, all the way down the hill until she reached the road that followed the river. On one side of the river was a hill that had been bare of life since the early industrial revolution, no trees grew on it, or shrubs, or wild flowers, only low growing mosses and scrub grass survived. On the opposite bank, spreading out over the flat expanse of the valley were old and new industrial warehouses, factories and work plants. Pipes jutted out over the river, disgorging waste products of a disturbingly vivid range of rainbow hues directly into the river. Here was a plastic factory where many of her charges would begin their working lives. Might they one day, she used to wonder, stand on their production line as they fitted the millionth plastic handle to the millionth plastic bucket, nourish themselves with lines of literature first heard from her lips in her classroom?

As I was young and easy, water, water everywhere, but not a drop to drink, it droppeth as the gentle rain from heaven, hubble bubble and a host of golden daffodils and do you remember an inn, Miranda?

The deputy head and Mr Roberts were pushing through the glass doors, laughing and talking loudly, she heard a trace of their conversation. 'And I said to her "if I wear that mackintosh to the club they'll mistake me for Harold Wilson".'

She started up the stairs to her left, one hand gripping the red plastic strip that covered the metal rail. The two men did not notice her, either that or they ignored her.

Over the stairs was a reproduction of a Picasso painting from his Blue Period. A blind and emaciated musician hunched over a guitar. It was yet another declaration of the school's modernity that at first sight had uplifted her. Now she found that she had seen so many children stream past it, never looking up, never acknowledging the picture, that she found herself loathing it.

She hurried down the corridor and unlocked her classroom, sat behind her desk at the front of the class and stared at the rows of desks and chairs before her.

It was in her mind to get a sheet of the school's headed notepaper from the supply in her desk, uncap her fountain pen and write a letter of resignation.

'Dear Sir, It is with regret that I find myself unable to continue in my post as a teacher in this great carbuncle of a school. I find I have grown to hate every single one of my pupils (an emotion I daresay they share with and towards me). Furthermore I hate every other member of staff from the lowliest – that obnoxious dinner lady, Mrs Cox who must surely have been concocted straight out of one of Charles Dickens' books with her dripping nose and boils and quaint phrases, to the highest, namely that obsequious and pompous and self-serving little twerp the deputy head. Another distressing development is that I have also grown to hate my subject: literature itself, I hate Walter de la Mare and Dylan bloody Thomas, and George Orwell and Coleridge. I despise Chaucer and want to piss on Shakespeare's grave. I'd strangle any living poet given half the chance. Send me Philip Larkin or WH Auden or Ted crowface Hughes and I'll soon stop them squawking and scribbling, I'll cut the fucking green fuse that feeds the fucking flower!'

She had a rich supply of vile language, those old Anglo Saxon words describing the body or its functions, but none had ever passed her lips. Not ever. They had swarmed in her mind at moments like these like a vast array of monstrous creatures, a slug with razor-sharp teeth, a wasp with claws that gripped its victims as he stung and stung again, an eel, a rat, a spider, a side-scuttling crab.

What was it her father had always said of people who swore or blasphemed – that it showed a lack of both imagination and vocabulary? As usual the memory of her father took on an almost tangible form and he often seemed to stand behind her just out of sight, always watching, always judging her.

The day after her father's funeral she'd gone to London with Tony Labruzzo to see a production of 'Look Back in Anger' and afterward they had stayed in a shabby Paddington hotel. What an accumulation of sins that had been! Tony was Italian and Catholic, they were unmarried, had watched a play her father would have called disgusting, eaten a Chinese meal in Soho, drunk beer in a public house called The Cambridge, then smuggled a bottle of cheap Spanish wine into their room where Tony had prised the cork from the bottle with a pen knife.

The wine was like vinegar, but she'd sloshed it into the tooth mug, forced herself to swallow it.

Was it courage she'd sought that night or oblivion? She'd wanted to be drunk enough to allow Tony to seduce her. To take her. To fuck her. Weren't Italian men like that? All beasts, as her father put it. According to her father and his

72

friends the entire male population of the world from Asia to Africa, from Tokyo to Tierra del Fuego; every Eskimo and Aborigine and Chinaman and Jew and wild Red Indian was just boiling over with lust for a white woman like her.

Not Tony though. When she woke the next morning she had only fleeting memories of what happened the night before, herself trying to dance a striptease and stumbling. Then when they were in bed, Tony pushing her away, saying, 'Not like this'. Then another flash, herself on her knees throwing up into the toilet bowl. Him saying, 'I don't know you.'

In the morning her mouth was dry and her head throbbed, there were particles of vomit in her hair, she stank.

She was alone in the bed, alone in the room, in the hotel, in London, in the world. There was a towel underneath her head, another at the foot of the bed. She wrapped herself up in the larger one and hurried to the bathroom where she locked herself in. She drank noisily from the tap and splashed water on her face. Turned on the bath to find only lukewarm water sputtered forth. She was certain he had left without her. He had probably left last night and got the mail train back to Wales. It was only what she deserved.

But just as her thoughts took even darker turns towards the idea of never returning to Wales, or worse, to suicide, she saw that on the shelf beside the sink Tony had left his toilet bag. She unzipped it, initially in search of toothpaste. Her own toiletries had not yet been unpacked; another sign of how drunk she had been, how utterly unlike herself.

He must have been in such a hurry that he forgot his wash things. There was his safety razor, his stick of shaving soap, his toothbrush case, a tube of Gibbs SR toothpaste, Old Spice aftershave with its picture of an old-fashioned sailing ship. There was a leather case that must contain a manicure set. His hands, his nails in particular were always immaculate, just as her father's always were. Easy enough if you weren't a manual labourer. She squeezed a line of the toothpaste onto her finger and rubbed it on her teeth, swished water round her mouth, spat and repeated the process until the worst of the taste and smell had gone. Replacing the tube, her eye was caught by a small leather box in his wash bag. It was small and square and burgundy coloured. She immediately knew it was a ring case and a new one at that. She stared at it certain that she was imagining it but knowing she would have to reach for it, open it and see whatever was inside it.

She was Pandora. She was Gretel breaking off a piece of the witch's gingerbread house, she was Persephone eating pomegranate seeds, she was Sleeping Beauty reaching with the tip of her finger to touch the needle that brings death, she was Alice falling endlessly.

She pressed the small gilt catch and the lid sprang up. Inside, nestled on its velvet perch was an engagement ring, a narrow band of gold with a decent sized single diamond. She snapped the case shut again, zipped up the wash bag, caught sight of her expression in the clouded mirror, saw not herself but Medusa, her mouth open in horror, her eyes registering terror.

She climbed into the bath and washed herself viciously, dipping her head under the water, loosening half digested rice, meat and carrots from her knotted hair with her fingers.

When she was done she pulled the plug and as a last

punishment she poured jug after jug of cold water over her head, down her back, her belly, her legs. Then naked and shivering she rinsed out the bath and poked the last fragments of last night's happiness down the plughole, off-white, orange and brown.

With one towel on her head and another wound around her body barely covering her, she opened the bathroom door and took at least four steps into the room before she saw Tony.

He was sitting in the Lloyd Loom chair by the window reading *The Daily Sketch*.

'Tony!' she said.

Not looking at her, he said, 'I got you some Alka Seltzer. I daresay you need some.'

'Thank you.' She felt compelled to take some immediately. She took the small tin, the tooth mug and bending awkwardly, collected her clothes from the floor where she must have scattered them the night before.

In the bathroom she dressed quickly, then briskly rubbed her hair, before filling the mug with water and adding the salts; drinking some, gagging, then drinking some more.

It crossed her mind to look at the ring again. The diamond had been larger than the one in her mother's engagement ring, but then her mother's had been one of three.

A sharp rap sounded at the door. Tony called out, 'We've got to leave in fifteen minutes if we're to catch the twelve o'clock train.'

He held her elbow as she climbed onto the train and lifted her overnight bag into the luggage rack for her. The compartment they were in was full, there was a man in a pinstriped suit and bowler hat, another older man with a waxed moustache, plus-fours and a copy of Wisden's, a pale young woman with two children who were obviously not her own, and a young soldier dressed in khaki. The last of these got out at Swindon, leaving her and Tony alone. He had spent the entire journey engrossed in first *The Sketch*, then *The Times* and finally a copy of *Reader's Digest* left behind on one of the seats.

She stared at him, willing him to look at her.

He frowned and chewed the end of his pencil, she moved to sit beside him. He was Testing His Word Power by filling in the magazine's regular vocabulary quiz.

'Ah, "eremite," she read from the page, 'that's a hermit isn't it? Or is it D. an educated person?'

It was the last but one question on the page and he had already circled the other answers, but now instead of acknowledging her, he closed the magazine and put it aside.

'Tony?' she said.

He closed his eyes, leaving her to gaze at his beautiful face and wonder when he might forgive her.

When they reached Swansea, he once again lifted her bag from the luggage rack and took her hand as she stepped down from the train, but then he set off down the platform at a brisk pace. She hurried to keep up with him, almost running at one point until at last she had to stop. Catching her breath, she watched as the distance between them grew until he passed the barriers and, without a backward glance, went out of sight.

She never saw him again, which as time went by, she considered a sort of mercy. Never again would his eyes pass coldly through her, never again would she confront the man who represented an entirely different life for her;

one with marriage and children and a modest home. She began to imagine that none of it had been real, there had never been a Tony, no giddy walk through the narrow streets of Chinatown, no vulgar kissing on the rattling Central Line, no engagement ring hidden in a rubberised wash bag.

And now just as she was beginning to think of herself as a creature who was hermetically sealed off from the physical body; a mind which experienced all of life through reading and thought alone; now when her maturity should signal to men not sexuality but respect; *now* she had been assaulted; touched by the vile, intrusive, no doubt filthy fingers of the roughest, most common, most despicable man she had ever had the misfortune to set her eyes on.

She glanced at her watch, half an hour had slipped away and she had neither fled the school, nor written a letter of resignation, nor prepared the first lesson. From her briefcase she snatched the poetry book she'd bought three years before. A gift for that self that hides within this disappointed woman; this husk, she thought bitterly.

She will read one of these verses by Sylvia Plath to Class 3C. These poems of the night, of death and darkness and spite. Flicking through she sees word after word of taboo – bastard, eunuchs, schizophrenic, crap and puke, fatso, a lecher's kiss, breast and womb, masturbating.

She turns the page and in the nick of time finds one poem that is sterile and opaque enough for her to mask her despair. She hurries to the office, makes copies and is back behind her desk, giddy and trembling as her blood sugar levels plummet.

And now the children are here, flowing into the veins of the school like the vibrii of cholera, pressing at the

77

classroom door, bodiless heads behind the square of glass, gaping dully.

The bell rings. The day begins.

WORD MADE FLESH

Sleepless I am. 'Tis as if the moon's broad face was leaning over me whispering softly, 'Wake up, Molly! Come on Molly Finnegan, you've work to do.' Then I must get up, slipping my feet into a pair of the old man's socks, wrapping a soft warm shawl around my shoulders.

This big old house is lonely by day but at night, though still alone, I feel myself to be its mistress. Those first sleepless nights I was cautious, creeping down to the kitchen only to steal a cup of water or a crust of bread, never lighting a candle, never opening any door but those I really needed to. After a month or so there came a night when, my hands numb and shivering with the cold, I dropped a tin jug on the flagstone floor. Such a crash it made, falling then rolling along with a resounding rattle. I was certain he would cry out, 'Who's there!' and come running downstairs to discover me. I stood stock-still wondering whether I should hide or pretend sickness. In the one case he might raise the alarm and then the constable would find me, in the other he might fear contagion, and many a servant has been turned out onto the street even on the brink of death. Or so I am told. No, I thought, I shall simply say I am very thirsty. Hang my head in shame. Fall to my knees and beg the master's forgiveness. Ask that he do anything, beat me or dock my pay, anything but send me from his door.

Such were the urgent plans that went through my head as I stood there trembling, my heart thudding in my breast, my breath coming and going as loud as the winter wind on the shore at Rosses Point. Or so it seemed.

Tick tock tick went the big grandfather clock in the hall. No creak of bedsprings came, no step sounded from above. Tick tock, then click, as the two hands of the clock met at twelve and the gears of the mechanism seemed to draw a rusty breath. Then bing bong, bing bong it rang out, bing bong bing bong. Then twelve sonorous bongs to mark the hour, so loud that I imagined all the dead who lay in their graves beyond the window would stir and rise to shake their ghastly fists at me.

But there was nothing. Only the moon winking through the beech trees and an old owl crying out, twit twoo.

That was a long time ago and suffice to say I have since lost my caution in my nightly jaunts for it is clear that my master, the Reverend Thomas Beynon, is a very sound sleeper. Let cats shriek and caterwaul and he will sleep on. Let lightning send its brilliant flashes over his lidded eyes, let thunder crash and wind roar. Let the barn over yonder catch fire, as it did this last summer, for the straw was as dry as tinder. Let all the village folk call and cry and run or ride by upon galloping horses. Let old Mrs Cadwalader beat upon an iron saucepan with an enormous spoon as she screams in her high-pitched Welsh, 'Tân! Tân!' Let five stout men, miners all, come clattering up the path to our yard and let them work the rusty pump and rattle their buckets and swear in four different languages, Welsh, English, Spanish and Italian. Let the church bells ring out and dogs howl and still he will sleep.

'Sleep well, did you sir?' I said that morning after the fire.

'Moderate,' said he with that weary note of complaint that is always in his voice. 'I don't sleep well as you know, for my burden is great and the troubles of my flock keep me from rest.'

'Indeed sir,' said I. 'A learned mind such as yours must be like a great fire that glows with hot embers long after the flame has died away.'

'Yes. Yes. Now, is my porridge ready?' he says craning his head toward the stove in anticipation.

He never really listens to anything I say. I can see it in his eyes which though seemingly distant are really inward looking. He thinks only of himself and expecting only trivial matters from my lips he does not pay attention. He might as well be listening to a cat. Or a dog. Or a pig. Or the chattering of starlings.

Later that morning he comes into the kitchen to tell me that the Cadwaladers' barn is naught but a heap of blackened timbers.

'You must have slept all through the noise and alarm,' says he, shaking his head ruefully.

I said nothing.

'We will pray for them and get up a subscription for the rebuilding of their barn.'

He pours cream from the jug over his porridge then adds a generous sprinkling of sugar. Smacks his lips. 'I think a boiled egg, Molly, will see me through this difficult morning.'

All his days are difficult. Every day is fought with his brave soldiering. Armed with a knife and fork he fearlessly slays the bacon, the sausages, the oxtail, the tongue and kidneys and chitterlings.

'Just a morsel I'll take, only to keep my strength up,' says he.

''Tis black pudding you'll be wanting for strength,' I say

and look at him, awaiting an answer. Then as encouragement I add, 'The blood, sir, is said to a source of...'

'Yes, yes. Though black pudding always wants bacon to set it off and make it palatable...'

To look at him you'd never think he ate so well for he is close to six foot but as thin as a boy of twelve. All legs, all neck, narrow shoulders and long arms that seem weighed down by wrists as big as goose eggs and hands that seem far too long to belong to him, but with fingers that must have been made for a gigantic woman, for they are finely formed and tapered yet so big even he hardly seems to know what to do with them.

Then there is his great beard, white it is and soft as downy feathers, he hardly ever cuts it and it hangs from his face reaching halfway down his sunken chest and sometimes you might see a bit of egg yolk dried in it. Or gravy. Or pie crust.

'You've food in your beard, sir,' I say. But as I said, often a time he doesn't listen to me and off he goes to disgrace himself in the pulpit, threatening hellfire and damnation with bits of cabbage stuck to his front teeth, gravy in his moustache and raisins falling from him onto the prayer book like manna from heaven.

I came here to be his servant as a girl of fourteen in 1851 and it's nigh on another fourteen years since then. So I figure half my life in Ireland half in Wales must fix me somewhere in the sea between.

I think my sleeplessness began back in The Great Hunger. You could tire yourself out with work by pulling a plough that's meant for a horse or building a road from nowhere to nowhere and you might fall asleep half-dead on a rough pallet, but your empty belly will wake you with its gripes and hollow torments.

I left Ireland on a ship piled high with grain and livestock bound for the mainland. We named her *The Good Ship Irony* and laughed though 'twas more for the sake of boldness as we were all full of fear for the future.

Yes, I'm certain that's when it began, my wakefulness. The first few weeks in Wales I just lay in my bed willing myself to sleep, tossing and turning. Then as I said I began to get up and tiptoe downstairs so that I could have a bite to eat. But then there I was in the kitchen at two in the morning and wide awake. Ah, the weariness of dead time! It almost maddened me, the vast nothing in the middle of the night. Then at last taking my chance I opened the door to his library. As luck would have it the fire had not quite died away and I added a few dry sticks to it, then a lump or two of coal and away it went, blazing up a treat. I perused his bookshelves – he had a great number of religious works notably *Foxe's Book of Martyrs*. I merely thumbed that book's pages as such stuff is nothing to me.

The Reverend thinks I cannot read or write being a poor Irish girl, but I did my book learning in a hedge school as many of my countrymen and women do and so having my letters I spent many a long night reading.

Then came one bitter winter when the fire in the library had quite gone out and no coals or logs were set ready but were locked up in the coal shed. All the keys, except those for the wine cellar and the tantalus, were on a chain kept on a hook in the boot cupboard, but this night the master, being forgetful, had not returned them to their rightful place. I searched but could not find them. By then I was chilled to the bone and my teeth were chattering.

I remembered that earlier, after he had locked the back

door, he went to wind the clocks. He was distracted, muttering to himself the first lines of the sermon he was composing. 'When the moon turns to blood,' he said. Then, 'A blood moon will come.' His voice with that quaver in it that he uses for his sermonising.

As a rule he'll wind the clocks, put those keys in his pocket, then lock the doors. 'The auld fool,' I thought. 'He's put all the keys in his breeches.'

I went upstairs and very quietly opened the door to his room, thinking to find the keys but in the dark it was hopeless. On he slept. He did not snore but I could hear the slow rhythm of his breath and see the rise and fall of his shoulder under the white sheets. He has an eiderdown on his bed and lovely cotton linens and woollen blankets. How I envied him then for the peace and comfort of his childlike slumber. I remembered that terrible winter of 1847 and how for warmth even strangers huddled close to one another. Like sheep will do in bitter weather and are we not all the Good Lord's flock, I said to myself, are we not all His poor creatures cast out of Eden?

I crept closer to his bed and gently lifted the covers and crawled under, settling into that space beside him where a wife would sleep. But it was cold, the sheets like a thin crust of ice. I shivered, then wriggled closer and closer again. He was curled up with his back to me, in the dim light I made out the pale knots of his back bone, the white wings of his shoulder blades. Naked he was. As shamefully naked as the day he had been born! I'd have been less surprised to find him in a hair shirt or even his holy vestments!

Even under the covers I suffered and trembled. And still he slept.

He slept and I wriggled closer for, like a moth attracted

to the light of a candle, I was compelled towards any source of warmth.

For a man I had always conceived as being like a stone, his heat, once his flesh was against me, was very great. I fitted myself in behind him, my face against his neck, my breasts against his back, my knees drawn up into his knees, my feet under the length of his feet. Quickly his heat passed into my body and the shivering fell away. I was like butter left out in the sun; I melted into him and must, very quickly, have fallen asleep, which had never been my intent.

I woke as dawn was breaking with a last beautiful dream of a summer's day still sweetening my mind with its scents of new-mown hay and summer stocks.

As luck would have it he hadn't woken before me and I rose and hurried away to my room to dress, then I returned straightway to rouse him as there was still the matter of the lost keys without which there would be no fire, no tea or porridge, no hot water for washing.

The following night was even colder and while there was coal aplenty to be had I found myself hankering after the plump eiderdown and fine sheets, and the man himself a great oven throwing off his warmth like a sun. So into his bed I got once more.

This went on all through that harsh winter and into spring when I at last gave up my nightly invasions.

The man himself was unchanged except that on the day in early May after the first night he had slept alone in nigh on six months, he complained of bad dreams in which Hell turned out to be a very cold and unpopulated place, not the busy furnace he'd always believed it to be.

'It's very disturbing to me, Molly. Do you think I'm sickening for something?'

'You are sickening for a wife,' said I.

But he did not hear me.

Through June, July and August he seemed more miserable than ever, even his appetite fell away and of an evening he took to drinking a medicinal draft of brandy, followed by tincture of laudanum.

By October the temperature had dropped and there was frost. I had spent my wakeful summer nights in reading *Robinson Crusoe, The Heart of Midlothian* and *Mansfield Park* and very happy that made me, but now here was the cold again wrapping its chill fingers over me like a wraith. Hardly thinking of it really, up the stairs I went and boldly into the Reverend's room and bed.

He was moaning very pitifully as I drew close to him, whimpering like a frightened pup. 'Those terrible barren dreams,' I thought. 'They still torment him.' But then as I pressed myself into him the noise stopped. 'Oh, blessed mother of Jesus!' I thought, 'I've woken him.' But no, his breathing lengthened and slowed and he, shifting a little, seemed to snuggle closer.

In late October the weather grew unusually warm; lady-birds settled on the windows and some shrubs began to grow buds, yet pitying the man I did not leave off my nightly incursion but crept into his bed and slept beside him, always rising before him at dawn.

I had always missed the old country, but my family now all being dead or scattered to the far ends of the Earth, I found comfort in the religion of my youth; which I confess I had abandoned, converting to the Protestant faith as a girl of twelve so that I could at last attend school. I was the only country cousin in my class, one of only three converts in the entire establishment and I was treated so cruelly by teachers and girls alike that after just six months I left. Then I worked in a hotel doing the most menial of tasks until I had saved enough money to bring me across on a boat to the mainland and thence to my current position. At the interview I was asked my religion and I gave it as Church of Ireland which was how it stood on paper no matter how it was in my heart.

I have a few Mass cards that I keep hidden under my mattress and twice in these fourteen years the Reverend has sent me alone to Newport to buy certain items he cannot obtain here and so I have twice gone to confession at St Mary's, but not since I took up my secret cohabitation of his bed.

'Is it a sin?' I wonder. A venial sin, for it cannot be a mortal one. I do not know him carnally and I do not covet him. It is only the mutual grace of our innocent slumber, that precious human warmth given surely by God for our comfort.

When next I go to Newport I will ask the priest there about this matter and pray he does not make me promise to stop. In the meantime Christmastide draws closer and as I go about my tasks I replay the Masses of my youth. I picture myself arriving at the church, dipping my fingers in the holy water and making the sacred sign of the cross. And there is my mother, her cheeks are rosy with the cold and in her arms she carries my youngest sister, Concepta. Here is Daddy standing tall with his cloth cap in one hand and the two boys, Brandon and Cormac hanging onto his other hand, two fingers a piece. And look, already sitting in the pew are Fenella and Aileen, my two beautiful older sisters and beside them there's Finbar, the handsomest boy in the county of Sligo and my own darling brother.

Now the altar boys come swinging the smoking incense, and we kneel and stand and sit and cross ourselves and kneel and pray. Then the priest opens his mouth and his lips move but no sound comes…

No sound comes because I have forgotten the Latin words.

No sound comes because Mammy and Daddy are dead and so are Concepta and Aileen. Finbar is in America with Brandon. Cormac's on the high seas off Nantucket, a red-haired Jack Tar. No one knows where Fenella went.

No sound.

I stop what I am doing, drop the scrubbing brush into the bucket and close my eyes where I am, kneeling on the tiles in the passage. I search my mind in vain, but nothing comes to me.

I am filled with an unbearable sadness that feels like a thousand weights attached to me by as many fish hooks. Or perhaps the sadness is all around me like the sea that traps a drowning man, sooner or later my mouth will open as his will, and all the pain will rush into my mouth and down my throat filling my lungs, destroying my life.

Days go by like this. I scrub the steps of the church, clean the grate and light the fire and during the service I try to join in the singing of hymns but the Welsh tongue, except for the odd word or two, is alien to me and that is another sadness.

The day before Christmas Eve I go to the meeting house as I am bidden. The women of the village want vases of holly on display as the berries are plentiful this year. They have cut the branches and left them heaped in the entrance, so I gather these up and carry them in, a great bundle of glossy green leaves and ruby berries. I go to the raised dias where the Reverend's Windsor chair stands by the simple pine table. I am struck as always by the lack of ornament; where are the gold candlesticks, the richly embroidered cloths of silver and satin, the high altar, the crucified Christ with beads of blood at his head, his ribs, his hands, his feet? Where are the ranks of candles each one lit in prayer? Why is the air not perfumed by incense?

I lay the holly on the table and go in search of some vases, there is a cupboard in the vestry and in it I find them, sure enough; put away with dying blooms and water still in them. I tip them into the sink and as the rotting stems fall I remember the stench of the blighted potato fields back home, the black putrefying mess that stretched as far as the eye could see.

'Oh, but we are a cursed people!' my mother had cried more than once, and I felt the curse upon me then, but my curse was the curse of escape, as I was cast out as surely as Cain had been.

I almost wept but fought it, ruthlessly scrubbing the vases before filling them with water and then holly. I worked so furiously the holly's sharp spikes caught my hands and arms, drawing pinpricks of blood to the surface.

When all was done I hurried back to the house to make the Reverend's tea, my mind now turning upon the most shameful of thoughts; that having no place in this world I should destroy myself and hope that God might send me to purgatory rather than straight to Hell!

That evening I served the master a good Irish stew of neck of mutton that he says is cawl and not Irish at all.

'Are we allowed nothing!' I said to him in a fury.

'Delicious!' said he, wiping his bread over the nearly empty bowl.

I get up violently, pushing my chair back so that it tips and crashes to the floor, then I run from the room and out of the house. I think I heard him say 'Molly?' but that is unlikely in truth.

I roam amongst the tombstones that surround the meeting house and as it is not quite completely dark, I read the names on the granite tombs and wooden crosses. I don't know why, perhaps I am still searching for Fenella.

A group of poor children pass just beyond the wall, they are singing as they go, the German carol 'Silent Night'. They wear layer upon layer of clothes, men's jackets with ragged sleeves turned back and belts or string around the waist, and long scarves knitted from scraps of wool, the girls in red flannel petticoats with check shawls over their heads. All had hobnailed boots that clattered and echoed on the cobbles. I watched them as they went, envying their little community, their joyful solemn song. None of them noticed me but when I said Fenella's name very low, almost soundlessly, one child stopped and looked me straight in the eye. Wisps of pale hair escaped from under the knitted hat she wore, her face was luminous like an Italian marble. A ghost child, I thought, but then she smiled and skipped away very prettily to catch up with the others. I stayed where I was for a very long time looking up the road where the children had disappeared, certain they would return. An hour, perhaps two, passed like this, then the cold drove me back indoors.

As I returned to the house, my mind seemed suddenly cleansed. At the door I turned my gaze upward to the great cloudless canopy of blackness and the eternal stars. Are they watching me, I wondered, all of my family and all of the saints? Then it came to me, the Mass sung at midnight, what Daddy called the Christmas Preface. The Latin words half-sung half-chanted by the priest, 'Quia per incarnate verbi mysterium.'

I held it in my mind, turning it over and round and through, repeating it in all its mystery and glory. These words should never escape again, I thought, I will store them in my heart and pump them round my body deep and red in my blood. This is my truth and my light.

I saw that the Reverend had already gone up to bed; that in the dining room my chair had been righted and the soup bowls removed. He would dismiss me from his service in the morning I was sure. Perhaps from Christian charity he'd let me remain until after Christmas, but I would surely be cast out.

'Quia per incarnate verbi mysterium.'

In the kitchen on the table I found he'd left a folded sheet of paper propped against the bread crock. My name on it.

Molly.

My fingers trembled as I picked it up. This must be the letter of my dismissal and no wages left with it. Not a single farthing. Where would I go? What would I do? What dark crevice of sin would catch me? Should I starve or become a fallen woman?

Verbi mysterium. Quia per incarnate.

I opened the paper, my eyes already swimming with tears that blurred my vision and made spangles of each flame in the room. The paper was almost empty except at the centre inside the fold were three words.

Don't leave me.

It was his handwriting yet still I feared some mischief for I had always thought of myself as invisible to the man.

Don't leave me. Verbi mysterium.

I sat for a long time by the fire, barely moving, hardly thinking, yet at the same time it seemed that a swarm of bees danced and hummed in my head.

At last the fire was reduced to a few embers and it was past midnight. I went up the stairs and into his room, not even changing into my nightgown first. I undressed taking off my brown wool frock, my flannel petticoat and vest and stays and camisole and stockings. Naked I was. As Eve had been. And innocent.

I lifted the covers, glimpsing my Adam's back, pale and naked, before I settled in beside him, pressing my flesh against his flesh and softly whispering, 'Quia per incarnate verbi mysterium', over and over until at last sleep overcame me.

I awoke at first light to find that in the night he had turned towards me and his arm was thrown over me and his leg was hooked over my legs and his head was nestled in my bosom. I wriggled to free myself and he stirred in his sleep and muttered some words into the pillow that seemed familiar yet I could not quite decipher them.

I tiptoed over to the chair and gathered up my clothes in a bundle then went to the door meaning to slip back to my own room to dress. The door creaked as I opened it but under that noise I swear I heard my name whispered in a quick and urgent appeal, 'Molly!'

I did not turn towards the sound afraid that I should see the old man's eyes open and feasting upon me with lust as in the bible story of Susanna.

Most of that day I kept to the kitchen and he to the library and in the evening I feigned sickness in order that I might avoid the Christmas service so I did not see what happened. Did not hear the poor man, in a wretched state of confusion, speak the Latin Mass. Had I been there all eyes might have turned to me accusingly, in older times his pious congregation might have burned me for a witch.

I left the next day and made my way to Cardiff where I found work in a temperance hotel.

Some time later I chanced to meet one of the miners from the village. His wife recognised me and was keen to talk.

'Well now,' she said. 'You've heard the news?'

'No,' said I.

'Old Thomas Beynon only lasted a week and a day after you left.'

'Wasted away to nothing he did.'

'Dew! He always was very thin though!'

'Well, after the funny turn he'd had that Christmas...'

They chattered on but I no longer listened to their words. Instead I heard a sound like the sea in a shell, a distant lonely murmuration, that must have been like the emptiness of his nightmares, for in his lonely sleep he had discovered that Hell was a cold and barren place to be cast out for eternity.

WHOSE STORY IS THIS ANYWAY?

That next day, a Saturday, a black-bordered envelope came in the post. Moth's great aunt Audrey had died. The funeral was in Brighton the following Wednesday. Moth, whose real name was Mary Olivia Theresa Hazeldine, had spent many unhappy summers living with her aunt after her father had disappeared in 1947.

She spent the afternoon shopping on Ealing Broadway for funeral wear. It was harder than one might have thought finding black clothes as that year navy was all the rage, but eventually she settled on a simple sheath dress in black with white polka dots, black court shoes and a single strand necklace of seed pearls. When she looked in the changing room mirror she saw someone who might have starred in a Hitchcock film (though she had never seen a Hitchcock film, only the photographs of scenes in the display case outside the cinema). To hide her dry (if not cold and triumphant) eyes she bought a pair of sunglasses with large squarish lenses and tortoiseshell rims and a black silk head-scarf. Jackie O, she thought. Or maybe that infamous girl, Christine Keeler, ducking into court, the elements of disguise hiding not grief, but guilt.

At Victoria, a guard, mistakenly and with the great courtesy of not inspecting her ticket, opened the door to the first-class carriage and she, not wishing to embarrass him, sat down and arranged herself elegantly in the window seat. The carriage was almost empty; dotted here and there were men in suits who tinkered with paperwork and whose cuffs were uniformly clean and crisp. She checked her watch and then retrieved a slip of paper from her handbag to review her booking at the Grand Hotel as well as the time and address of the funeral.

The train began to move slowly, when it had picked up a little speed, the door to her carriage opened and on a faint air of London must, a man blew in and sat in a flurry of mackintosh and briefcase and newspaper in the seat opposite hers. He seemed not to have noticed that she was already occupying that table, or that the one across the aisle was empty. She saw him do a double take when he noticed her; his eyes, large with surprise, went from her to the other free seats, to the heap of possessions he'd thrown beside him. Then he shook his head, smiled to himself and looked directly at her.

'Do you mind?'

Moth took off her dark glasses. 'No, of course not.' She placed the glasses in their case, arranged the slip of paper so that it was perfectly aligned with the case.

'That's where I'm staying – The Grand,' he said. Then, seeing her alarmed expression he added, 'Sorry. That was rather impertinent, wasn't it?'

'Well…' she said, uncertain whether to tick him off or accept the apology.

'Business trip?' he said, his eyes seeming to swarm from her face to her bosom to the slip of paper in front of her.

Before he could read the details of the funeral, she folded the note and put it back in a zippered compartment in her bag.

'Yes.'

'We could share a taxi to the hotel,' he said – very distinctly.

But somehow she heard, *We could share a room at the hotel.*

'I beg your pardon?'

'I'll pay, of course,' he added in all innocence.

'Good God,' she thought. 'He's mistaken me for a pros-titute!' But, trying to make a joke of it, said, 'Are you sure you can afford it?'

He laughed and patted the back of her hand. A deal had been struck it seemed.

Great Aunt Audrey used to say that Moth was sly, that she should be watched as she had 'come-to-bed' eyes.

He picked up his newspaper. Moth, replacing her dark glasses as if the sun were catching her eyes, took a good hard look at him. She guessed him to be in his mid to late thirties, trim and healthy looking. He had a good head of dark blond hair, no grey that she could see, a longish face and square chin, a modest nose, small mouth, with pale, flesh-coloured lips. Eyebrows and lashes that were darker than his hair.

As if he was suddenly aware of her gaze, he looked up and said brightly, 'Have you been to The Royal Pavilion?'

'Oh well, not since I was a child…'

'Never been! Not in all the years I've been coming down – can you believe that?'

'Well…'

'It's not the sort of thing you do on your own is it? I mean there should be someone with you, or else you'd look like an odd fish.'

His eyes were brown with flecks of gold, his teeth small, white and even.

'What do you think? Want to save a chap from looking like an odd fish?'

'I'm not sure.'

'Oh, say you will. We'll hop in a cab, drop our bags at the hotel, go straight to the Pavilion. Tell the boss the train was delayed, eh?'

The ticket inspector arrived. Her travelling companion reached into his inside pocket and presented his ticket, then both men turned to her. She took out her purse and without hesitation handed over her second-class ticket.

'You're in the wrong carriage. Plenty of seats in second,' the inspector said and indicated with a hand as stiff as a wooden signal the way out of the first-class compartment.

'Oh, for goodness sake, man! We'll be there in less than twenty minutes! You're surely not going to insist the lady move seats now?'

The guard muttered something that she did not hear as it seemed a shrill buzzing had filled her ears and her heart flapped like a fish on mud flats deep in the dark estuary of her chest.

'Let me pay the difference. I'm sure this is just some mistake on the part of the booking office. How much do you want for the lady?'

How much do you want for the lady? That was an odd way of putting it. Money passed between the two men, disappearing into the guard's pocket with seamless speed. No new ticket was issued.

Now she really had been bought, there was no getting away from it.

There was the funeral to consider. Two o'clock on Bear Road. The train got in at twelve-forty; she had planned a taxi to the hotel to drop off her bag, then back in the same cab to the service.

She had a picture of herself at the graveside, handfuls of

earth in her palm, then the soft stammering sound as they were cast on the coffin. Her come-to-bed eyes as dry as old bread crust behind the black insect eyes of her sunglasses.

Audrey had loved to talk about her own death, as if it were the fulcrum on which all good and evil depended. Moth grew very tired of the predictions flung at her by Audrey; 'You'll be sorry, you'll rue the day. When I'm gone, then you'll know!'

She had been thinking of this and gazing with a frown out of the window when she glimpsed the green swathes of The Downs rolling lyrically by.

'So ... the Pavilion?' the man said, smiling hopefully.

'I can't I'm afraid.'

'No?'

'I have an appointment I can't miss.'

'Later this afternoon, then? Tomorrow?'

'Hm ... maybe.'

'I see,' he said and seemed to withdraw into himself. He fussed with his newspaper, then hid behind it and pretended to be engrossed in it for the rest of the journey.

As they neared the station, he stood up and gathered his belongings and without another word made his way to the exit.

Outside the station she saw several taxis pull away and by the time she reached the rank none were waiting.

Convinced that she had done nothing to make him become so cold towards her she turned the whole episode over and over in her mind until she had rehashed it entirely from a romance into a melodrama so ensnaring and deceptive and deadly that she felt sure she was lucky to escape with her life. He was a killer, a sadistic rapist preying on the sort of woman who could afford a first–class ticket. He was in cahoots with the inspector. And as for that charade of him being the last to board the train and thus being so flustered he sat with her instead of at any of the other empty seats! Why, he'd probably been on the train long before her, sizing her up. All he had to do was open and close the door, then scurry distractedly up the aisle and throw himself down opposite.

But, given such an elaborate plot, why had he given it up so abruptly? She looked around her, half expecting to see him waiting for her, watching.

A cab drew up and the driver got out, popped the boot, came around the car and stooped to pick up her bag. Panicking she snatched it out of his reach.

'I've changed my mind,' she said imperiously. 'I'll walk.'

'Suit yer bleeding self, Mrs!' he called after her and she felt his anger like so many poisoned darts in her back. It was not a very long walk to the Grand on the seafront and her bags were not heavy; the key reason for getting a cab was timing. It was the matter of not only getting to the hotel but getting to the funeral on time.

Having marched at a furious pace down West Street, she now slowed, calculating not only the business of checking in, then finding another taxi, but also the fact of her whereabouts being known. He, or rather they – for he had his henchmen, would be waiting for her at the hotel, and despite the Grand's gracious reputation, it was very possible that a bell boy or kitchen porter was also in on the scheme.

Was this not what Audrey had always warned her about? 'When I'm gone, then you'll know!' and with this thought an even more elaborate plot was revealed to her in all its nail-biting horror, its vengeful calculation. All of this was Audrey's concoction; she had planned it from beyond the grave, hiring these men with her long-hoarded pounds, shillings and pence, in order to be proved unequivocally right with her bitter old predictions. To be certain to have the last word.

Or Audrey was not dead at all. Not yet. She was hovering on the brink, as enlivened by this last act of cruelty as Lazarus by the presence of Christ. This was her sanatorium of good air, this her penicillin, her youth–giving sacred fire.

No. Moth checked herself. It was too much. A flight of fancy as preposterous as those she'd had as a girl.

Such as when she had seen the strange man staring in at her from the window in Audrey's house and later smelled the smoke from his cigar drifting from Audrey's bedroom. The guest room and Audrey's bedroom were linked by a long balcony that overlooked the drive, the defunct fountain and the incorruptible lawns, and a man might easily have walked along it to spy on her.

'This child's imagination must be checked,' Audrey had instructed her mother sternly the next day. She had then gone on to offer such a terrible and detailed account of her mother's shortcomings as a parent that both Moth and her mother and the lady's companion whom Audrey had hired that year, a beautiful young TB sufferer called Helen, were all moved to crescendos of weeping.

Moth had been drawn to Helen – even her name carried the freight of tragedy – she was Helen Keller the blind, deaf and dumb girl, and Helen of Troy and Helen Burns, Jane Eyre's dearest friend who had died in her arms. Only once had Moth had the opportunity to be alone with Helen and that had been short-lived. She had wandered into the walled kitchen garden behind the house and found Helen collecting herbs for a tisane. Shyly, Moth had crept closer and closer and was rewarded with a friendly smile.

'Smell this,' said Helen and she rubbed a leaf between her fingers then offered it to Moth.

'Lemons!'

'That's lemon verbena. Here, what's this?'

'Lavender!'

'Good and this one?'

She let Moth cut some of the stems and showed her how she laid them neatly in rows at the bottom of the wooden trug. She explained their use in medicine and their symbolism; twelve sage leaves picked at midnight for divination, bay leaves to ward off evil, coriander as a love potion.

If a child is capable of falling deeply and everlastingly in love, then Moth fell into that beautiful condition at that moment. Add the drone of bees, the great aching canopy of intensely blue sky above, the pungent perfume of the flowers, the sun warming her pale and winter-starved skin, and Helen's kind but tragic beauty, and all becomes clear.

The sound of a cane rapped on a metal gate caused both of them to jump. Moth turned to see Audrey, her mouth set in a hard fleshless line, her eyes small and black and bright, her chin raised. Helen quickly rose to her feet and gathered up the scissors and the trug with hands that were visibly trembling. Audrey slowly raised the cane as if it were a divining rod set to sniff out evil then started toward them. Helen hurried off, ducking as she passed Audrey as though she expected the cane to fall upon her shoulders. Moth stood where she was, rigid with fear. She was seven years old.

She never dared approach Helen again, but looked at her

often with baleful helpless eyes. Helen avoided the child's gaze, her touch, the very breath from her lips – for *she had been warned*. Not long after that Helen was gone and never spoken of by anyone in the house again.

'Then you'll know!'

Moth seemed to hear the old woman's voice and sensed the whip-like shadow of her cane flickering impatiently like a branch against the moon. 'That child lets her imagination run riot. She is in mortal danger; the devil will find use for her and make no mistake!'

The song of Audrey's words was constant, a noise that went on echoing and ringing in the ears and mind long after the tongue had ceased its flapping.

What had she, Moth ever done to attract such suspicion? She had been far too young for the depravity and cunning of which she was accused, far too young to cast off the wolf's skin thrown upon her and see it as a thing apart. She was a lamb unbloodied in the ripe pasture of the world, and yet the weight of the predator's disguise crippled and disfigured her. She had no chance to grow up straight and tall and true, no matter how she strived after goodness.

There was no changing anything, the damage was done. A taxi was on its way up the road to the station, she waved to it and the driver made a u-turn causing another driver to blast his horn. This seemed to prove to her that an alteration in plans always created discord somewhere.

'To the Grand,' she said. 'Then on to Bear Road.'

He was not one of those chatty taxi drivers who felt compelled to discuss the weather or the state of the world. He had a set of beads hanging from his driver's mirror that she at first took for a rosary, then thought better of it, as his look, sallow skin and a great head of grey black curls told her otherwise. There was a photo fixed to his dashboard; dark-haired girls in brightly coloured party frocks, gathered around an older woman. She would have liked to have a conversation about these girls, ask how old they were now and did he also have sons and if not, was that a sorrow to him? But she had a way of turning such friendly queries into an interrogation, of setting a person on edge.

She ran into the hotel and gave her bag to reception as her room was not yet ready. She half expected to bump into the man from the train, but then he must be off, padding respectfully around the Royal Pavilion, standing behind a fat silky scarlet rope, peering at an elaborately curtained bed or columns topped with copper palm leaves. She should have gone with him, saved him from being – what had he said – an odd fish. Back in the cab, she fastened her seat belt and as the driver pulled off she said, 'Those are your daughters, I suppose.'

'They are no daughters of mine,' he said and shook his head, denying and disowning them with such vehemence, that she felt afraid.

She was entirely ignorant of the fact that certain taxi drivers shared their vehicles with others; that this man sat with these prayer beads and the photograph of the woman and her five nameless daughters day after day with no more relationship to them than to the steering wheel or the gear stick. Nor could she know that his English, still a strange meat on his tongue, had been half-learned from Shakespeare and Dickens as he sat beneath drying octopus in his father's taverna in Chania, Crete.

Her vision grew blurred as tears poured from her eyes and the unfamiliar streets seemed to flash past in a riddle.

She had no idea where she was, where he was taking her.

At last he slowed the engine. 'Bear Road,' he said. 'What number?'

A long row of houses stood on one side of the road with a featureless tall grey stone wall opposite. Above the wall the tops of trees could be seen, green and dense and giving no indication of what lay beyond.

'I don't know,' she said and thought, do cemeteries have numbers? Or churches? Or crematoriums? She opened her handbag to find the paper with all the details, but it was gone. He brought the car to a standstill and turning in his seat said, 'It's a long road.' A car honked its horn behind them and he drove a little further until he found a place to pull in. A long black hearse sailed majestically past, the coffin in the back engulfed by flowers. Four more gleaming limousines followed.

'It's a funeral,' she said. 'Follow them.'

He raised his hands in despair, but tagged onto the tail of the procession. Further up the road the cars turned one after another and poured through a wide gate in the wall.

The taxi followed pulling up behind a long line of cars. She paid the driver and instantly forgetting her distrust of him, tipped him generously. Gathering herself, smoothing her dress, she walked unsteadily towards the small black-clad gathering. People nodded at her or smiled the strange sad smiles of greeting reserved for funerals. Many of the mourners were youngish, smart and good looking; there was no one over fifty or sixty that she could see. Many of the people dabbed at their eyes or consoled one another with tender gestures; pats on the back, a hug, a long held handshake. More cars arrived, Bentleys and Wolseleys and Jaguars, disgorging another thirty or so people.

Moth felt a pinch of jealousy, if she died how many would attend her funeral? And what would they look like? A hodge podge, a rabble in fraying suits worn for weddings, christenings, job interviews and funerals for year after year, or not wearing black at all, but maroon, like her mother, who had only one good winter coat.

She turned to watch the men slide the coffin from the hearse and began to hear the name Freddie peppering the air around her in many conversations. Freddie or Frederick or darling Fred. Or poor Fred. Brave Fred. And it dawned on her: she was at the wrong funeral.

As the mourners made their way inside, Moth walked back to Bear Road. Once there she stopped and looked around, aghast. There were *three* cemeteries very close to one another, all with different names. How could this be? She had the sensation that someone was watching her confusion and discomfort, laughing behind their hand.

'*Then* you'll know.'

The words were always there. Then you'll *know*. Then *you'll* know.

'Know what?' she said angrily, her voice strange to her at this crossroad of death, so manicured and suburban under a blue afternoon sky. 'You never said, Audrey. What will I know?'

At the entrance gates she passed from the dazzling light into the shadow of the trees and found that she could barely see. She hesitated a moment uncertain of her direction, aching for all the lost opportunities of her life, and particularly the most recent. She saw herself in the cool rooms of the Royal Pavilion, a gentleman by her side, cupping her elbow as he pointed to some detail in the hand-painted wallpaper. Then stumbling blindly, desperate now to be gone she stepped into the road and straight into the path of the hearse bearing her aunt's coffin. The driver was late and as there were no cars following him he was driving at a less than stately pace.

Moth remembered now the beautiful chinoiserie wallpaper that must have lodged in some bright corner of her mind since childhood; a bird, the Paradise Flycatcher perhaps, rising up in the air in an explosion of energy and colour, its long tail feathers like gay, powder-blue ribbons. And she, Moth, flew up in air and only when she fell to earth did she finally know everything.

VELVET

Clive's wife had to leave before the foal was born. Dawn was breaking and the mare had been increasingly restless; its eyes rolling wildly as if in search of a cause for the mysterious agitation inside her body. The vet was there and the stable owner too, so they had no need of her presence, but she had wanted to see it happen. Witness the miracle of it, despite the blood which habitually made her queasy. She'd once seen a black and white film of a foal being born; the curious sight of those long gangly hard-hoofed legs, slick as hot butter slipping from the mother. But no, it was Julia's tenth birthday and there was the party to organise.

The tulips stood in straight lines, twelve inches apart in weed-free soil that was grey and dry and hard. One of the girls at the party looked at these tulips from time to time with an uncertain curiosity. Being ten years old she was unable to make a decision about the flowers. The house that the garden belonged to was older than her own and her house was in its turn older than those on the council estate where most of the girls at the party went to school. Julia, whose party it was, was always top of the class, read clever books, was never untidy or unruly, answered questions in class, and drew benevolent glances and words from the teacher as she sat straight-backed, her precise mouth opening and closing on perfectly enunciated words.

After the food, the sandwiches and crisps, the cake and jelly, the children had been ushered into the garden to play, but Julia had gathered six of the girls in the shed and excluded three others. Such a thing had never happened at a party before, the adults were meant to supervise everything, to organise games like musical chairs or pass the parcel, to hover nearby ensuring fairness.

The three excluded girls, dressed in their prettiest frocks and white knee-high socks and shiny patent shoes, wandered morosely about the garden, restless, uneasy and insulted. The heads of the taller girls could be glimpsed moving about inside the shed through the high square window, but whatever they were doing in there was unknowable. The interior of the shed itself seemed a tempting secret – it might have been filled with books and a writing desk, or every impressive toy and game, Sindy and Barbie and Tressy dolls standing in serried ranks near miniature plastic wardrobes stuffed with miniature clothes on miniature clothes hangers. All the shoes in rows and in pairs. Sindy's perfect duffle coat with its tiny wooden toggles, Barbie's air hostess uniform. There might have been a chemistry set in there. A microscope. A full-sized Dalek. An easel and real tubes of oil paint. A sewing machine. A typewriter. Endless sweets. A diskette record player (though no music could be heard).

One of the children banished from the shed was a strange girl who stayed at the periphery of everything, who had acquired a sort of invisibility; she bothered no one and no one bothered her. It was hardly a surprise that she was excluded from Julia's den, more surprising that she had been invited to the party at all. This exclusion was an alien experience for the other two, yet all three were caught in this no-man's-land. They were barred from Julia's inner sanctum and could not go back inside the house. The garden itself had few distractions, there was no swing or slide to play on, no rubber ball to throw or catch, no trees to climb or shrubs to hide behind, no rope to skip with.

The atmosphere of the house and garden, though the three girls could not have named it as such, was stark and oppressive. They were unwanted and under scrutiny, but there was no solidarity in this, they saw one another as shabby reflections of each other; this one strange, this one thin and poor with countless brothers and sisters who yet possessed an aura of goodness. This one with tangles in her hair and dirty, scabbed knees who was always in trouble, always naughty, but without guile or cruelty.

They lingered, or traipsed along the square path, tested the thin green lawn with its sharp blades of new grass, two of them staying together, while the third kept her quiet vigil at a distance. She might grow up to be a nun. Or a prostitute. Never quite of this world.

Storming the clubhouse was out of the question. They did not peer into its window, nor listen at its door. Nor yell nor kick at its creosoted timbers. They did not slip around the side of the house to knock at the kitchen door and complain to her mother that Julia had banned them from her clubhouse, for the mother was as austere as Julia herself, as cold and formal and judgmental with hair clipped short into a mannish helmet just like Julia's.

Each girl had arrived bearing a gift; toys or games chosen by their mothers, wrapped in pretty paper by them. The presents ensured safe passage over the river Styx and into the delights of the birthday party. To be excluded like this was a terrible thing.

Dull was the afternoon under the weak sun. Dull the featureless garden. Dull the windows of the house that reflected only the dull garden, the pale, cloud-threaded sky. Dull the joyless silence and the scrape of small feet on paving slabs or gravel. The only colour came from the tulips with their sturdy stems, their beautiful goblet-like flower heads, red and yellow and orange.

Experimentally one of the three girls crouched by the flowerbed in order to study one of the tulips more carefully. The stem looked thick and strong and straight with the flower head forming its cup exactly over the centre of the stalk. Perhaps it was this that gave her the idea for what she did next, because to all intents and purposes it looked like a sturdy container for something ... but what? Nearby in the dusty, dry-crusted earth she spied a small friendly pebble no larger than a regular marble. She picked it up and carefully, almost tenderly, dropped it into the tulip. The result was disappointing; she had wanted to see the stone nestled inside the flower, hunkering down among its complicated innards, its stamen, pistil and anther. No, the result was sudden and shocking. She let the pebble drop from her fingers and the tulip's head abandoned its ardent and lovely uprightness, snapped at the neck and fell onto the unyielding earth below.

In a different sort of garden, where banks of flowers grew in massed clumps, the damage might have passed without notice, but here, where the sparseness, the regimentation of their planting was absolute, the one decapitated stem was unmissable.

The girl somehow expected her crime to be immediately detected, for a scream of outrage to emanate from the woman in the house or from Julia in the shed or from one of the other two girls adrift in the raft of the garden. Or perhaps from the flower itself – a high warbling screech of pain: falsetto, indignant, accusing.

A boy might have set to work with glee deliberately meting out the same fate to all of the tulips, but a girl – a normal girl – was not meant to be on the side of destruction, especially the destruction of flowers.

She glanced around, saw no angry parent striding towards her, saw no furious girl mouthing accusations at her from the shed window, heard no furious cry. She picked up the flower head and tried to reattach it by balancing it on the stem, but it only fell again and again, bruising some petals and losing others. Giving this up she attempted a burial, but the ground was hard and unrelenting. Finally she chose flight, putting as much distance between herself and the crime scene as the modest garden would allow.

Julia's mother looked with fury at the dining table where her daughter and her guests had sat an hour before. The paper plates were littered with sandwich crusts and iced biscuits that had been licked clean, then abandoned. The cherryade Julia had insisted on having seemed to have been spilled everywhere in large and small pools on the white linen tablecloth. One of the Hepplewhite chairs which had only just been reupholstered at great cost had a worrying damp patch on the seat. Little beasts, she thought to herself, utter, utter beasts.

To make matters worse Mrs Brookes had refused to change her day and had cleaned the house yesterday as usual and would not be back until Friday. Well, once the little monsters had finally gone home, Julia would just have to clean up the mess herself. That was only fair. And one had to be fair, didn't one?

Trust Clive to be away this week of all weeks. Thinking of her husband, she turned sharply on her heel and hurried up the stairs, her court shoes tapping on the polished steps in a satisfying way. She found the key to her husband's study and let herself in as she did every couple of days or so. Sometimes she wondered if he knew she knew where he hid the key, if so that was just typical of him. She had seen that smug little smirk across the breakfast table once too often to take him at face value.

Everything looked just as it always did. His 'at home' pipe was in the ashtray, there was a clean sheet of blotting paper in its leather holder (she had in the past held a blotting sheet up to a mirror to decipher the royal blue hieroglyphs imprinted there). Benjamin Britten's *Peter Grimes* was on the gramophone turntable. A copy of *Wisden Cricketers' Almanack 1964* lay next to his armchair. Why was the cover yellow, she always thought, shouldn't it be green? She did not understand men.

If he knew she knew about the key, then what was the point?

She drifted to the window and was surprised to see a strange child sitting on the step near the coalhole. It was trying juggle three misshapen balls, or perhaps they were stones, throwing them high in the air, then tilting her head back to follow their flight in order to catch them. Wearing a dress that must have been made from an old pair of curtains, faded moss green velvet with a drooping sash. Cheap-looking imitation leather shoes. Off-white socks with wrinkles at the ankles. It looked grubby in some unseen and indefinable way.

She was about to bang on the window in order to shoo the wretched thing away when she remembered – Julia's party! Of course. How could she have forgotten!

But why on earth was this child on her own? Where was Julia? She was meant to keep an eye on her guests and make sure they did not misbehave.

Just then two more little girls came into view, walking slowly and by the look of it singing some nonsense or other as their mouths were opening and closing in unison.

Silly creatures. She much preferred horses. If she'd given birth to a foal instead of Julia she couldn't have been more delighted, but that sort of thing only happened to the Greeks or in fairy stories.

She left Clive's study not bothering to relock it, that would bloody well show him, wouldn't it? Clip clop down the stairs, briskly into the lounge and out through the French windows.

The creature on the step didn't even look up and the other two had their backs to her. Faintly she heard their surprisingly sweet voices mournfully singing, 'How-ow could you use a poor-or maiden so?'

A memory seemed to suddenly scorch her. Of herself when young. Of happiness; the sharp remembrance of a lighter heart.

Walking faster now, diagonal across the lawn, to the shed. Where else would that daughter of hers be? Trying the door, she found it locked and rattled it furiously. A flurry of shushing and shuffling erupted from inside, then silence. She slapped the door with the palm of her hand.

'Go away!' Not Julia's voice. No.

The two little girls who had been singing stood nearby

watching her, fascinated, their song frozen in the spring air.

She moved to the shed's window, peered in. She saw nothing at first, then perceived a figure lying prone on the floor wearing nothing but a pair of navy knickers. Several shiny heads of freshly washed hair encircled her. It looked satanic, the one girl lain out like a corpse, while the others kneeled over her. It took her breath away; she could not quite believe her eyes.

Then a scream made her turn her head. The two little girls who had been singing squealed together in a unified cry. There was the wretched creature in the velvet frock, blood pouring from her nose, down her face and the front of her dress, splashing the concrete path.

The two little girls who had been singing ran past her, drawn inexplicably to the one who was spouting so much blood. When they reached her one produced a hankie, while the other tipped the girl's head back and pinched the bridge of her nose. They did not seem to mind the blood.

Julia's mother hurried back inside the house locking the French doors behind her, then she sat on the loveseat and thought again about how the sky at dawn had been streaked with red and how the foal, within minutes of being born, would struggle to rise on brand new legs, and its hair, once dried in the sun, would look like velvet.

THE GREEN HOUR

She thought of the sea as her beating heart and so its violence on certain wild nights frightened her. On other days it seemed to have shrugged on a green cloak that rippled with shifting mysterious shadows. Despite this she was glad to leave the provincial Welsh town and join her brother in London. Later she'd gone to Toulouse with Dorelia McNeill and painted her standing by a table with a book in her hand, her lips the colour of coral, her hair like the black sea on a moonless night. They had meant to walk to Rome, but Gwen ended up in Paris, alone.

Auguste Rodin hired her as a model and to celebrate took her to the *café* for absinthe. *'L'heure verte, Marie,'* he said. He could not quite manage the, to him, alien name of Gwen so this is what she became. She watched as he let the water trickle, drop by slow drop through the cube of sugar and into the green spirit where a pale swirling cloud began to appear like a wraith.

She could not tell him that she'd had nothing to eat that day and nothing since breakfast the day before. The drink warmed her and then seemed to flood her body with energy. She had a second glass and stared intently at the brilliant green, thinking first of emeralds and jade, then cats' eyes.

He reminded her of her father. Except that her father's gaze came with a disapproving silence. When she was a girl it seemed that only the sea washing beyond the windows had broken the silence of the house in Tenby. That and the loud tick, tick, tick of the grandfather clock. She would escape to the sea and draw the wild urchin children; some, in the heat of summer, quite naked in the shallow lapping waves.

'The green hour,' she said in English, then smiled at his puzzled expression.

A third glass of absinthe. As the water entered the clear green liquid she thought about an old cat she'd once seen, its blind eyes clouded over, their colour muted.

'You have an athlete's body,' he said later when she stepped from behind the screen in the studio and slipped the robe from her shoulders. He approved of her slim hips, her slender legs, her small breasts; she would do very well for the sculpture he had in mind. He also had a seduction planned ... but then so did she.

He was 64. His beard was a great wiry nest, nearly white. She was reminded of the stuffed doves under the glass dome in the drawing room in Tenby. Gentle plump birds made still and silent by death.

She posed for him, taking up attitudes that exposed to him the most intimate parts of her body. This she gave for art first and secondly for love.

For love and against silence.

No, it was not his beard that reminded her of the stuffed doves, not really. It was his manhood. They had made love on the floor of the studio and he had rolled off her and lay back exhausted, spent, his eyes closed and an arm flung over his face. She let her gaze fall on his member where it seemed to nestle in a pale curve against his thigh and it was that which reminded her of the doves under the glass dome.

Time dripped by, water dissolving a sugar cube, sweetening the bitter wormwood and distorting the senses. He tired of her and abandoned her for another woman. Then further abandoned her by dying. She had a sense of belonging nowhere and to no one.

Except to God.

A sharp pain rippled through her belly. Was it the spot where a sword had been thrust into the body of Christ? She painted wet daubs of Rouge Phoenician on the palms of each hand. Stigmata. *No saint, she.* Then wiped them away on a turpentine-soaked rag.

What she lacked was the religion of ritual and confession. How bare and without passion was the church of her youth; the puritan sparsity, the chill incantations, the Sunday best clothes, the eyes of the congregation slipping sideways to see what coins a neighbour had placed on the collection plate.

She mixed ground barley with milk and drank it slowly over the course of half an hour. She was not sure if it worsened the pain, which seemed a constant, but it was all she could manage.

Often she thought of the sea. Once she had watched a child being lifted from the waves at Tenby's North Beach. Half drowned he'd been, the son of a blind piano tuner on holiday from Bristol, and when he recovered she saw him leading his father up the steps and towards the town. Her brother Augustus had nearly destroyed himself diving into the sea and dashing his head on the rocks when he was 18 or 19. People said he was different after that, especially with women.

One day in the Louvre she was crossing a gallery in search of paintings of Christ's wounds, when someone caught her eye. He was reflected in a glass cabinet. She stopped walking immediately, mesmerised. It was him, her master, Rodin, standing quite still and gazing over his shoulder as if he were as arrested by the sight of her as she was by him. For a moment she forgot the pain in her stomach, she forgot the painting she was trying to complete, everything in the world melted away. There he was again, her lover back from the dead after 22 years, come to claim her.

Then her senses caught up with her and she saw that this was no living, breathing man, but a statue. A sharp cramping pain ripped through her like a lightning bolt, almost taking her breath away, but she bore it bravely and made her way towards the cruelly deceptive sculpture.

Neptune, god of the sea. An ache sprang up in her heart, worse by far than the physical one in her stomach and it was followed by an impulse; she must go now, go back to the sea.

She caught the train to Dieppe. All the way in the cramped railway carriage, pain like the arrows that pierced the flesh of St Sebastian. Nothing to eat – only a cup of tepid water to wet her lips. Pain like a lance thrust into Christ. *This is my blood, this, my body...* Exquisite pain, as if to herald another world war.

In a quiet street not far from the station her knees buckled and she had to rest, clinging to a railing for support. A black Tomcat came strutting out of the dusty undergrowth, its tail raised high, quivering with pleasure. One of her own it must have been, come back to her as a ghost. Eyes so sharp, so green, so pure she could never replicate them; though her mind from habit seemed to trace a paintbrush over her palette from Cobalt to Terre Verte to Viridian; so many greens ... and the sea now so near she could almost smell it.

STORM DOGS

Pen y Cae, October 1949

Dorothy met him in the Ancient Briton not far from the small village where each of them had ancestors. She had deferred her place at Wellesley College for a year in order to see Europe and her maternal grandmother had given her fifty dollars and a camera; a black and silver Leica in a tan leather case. Then she had extracted a promise; Dodo must go to Wales, must take photos of the old farm, the mountain, the church, the gravestones of the Thomases, the Craddocks, the Vaughans and Dandos.

Everyone stared at her when she entered the pub; she had the sense that she had barged into someone's private living room, though the door had 'Public Bar' engraved on its glass. She stood out amongst the local women in her crisp sky-blue slacks, crew-necked sweater and saddle shoes. They seemed mired in the mud and heather, the tree bark and tea stains judging by the colours of their clothes, all of them in skirts and worn-looking winter coats and stout-looking dress shoes. Not that there were any women in the pub at midday.

He had approached her at once, handsome and smiling, making her feel welcome. He bought her a glass of warm beer. Then he had sung a haunting song in the language of his (and her) people. Everything had stopped in that moment, no one moved, no one touched their drink or

119

spoke or lit the cigarette that dangled from their lips. All eyes were on the black-haired young man as he leaned almost jauntily on his stick and lifted his head and voice to heaven.

When she said it was time for her to go, he walked her outside and asked if he could kiss her. She understood that he had been in the war, that his leg had been damaged by shrapnel or gunshot or mine. She said yes because she was ashamed to say no.

'Marry me!' he said and she laughed and skipped away out of reach.

An hour later she was on the mountain, faithfully taking the photos her grandmother had asked for, when she fainted. A sheepdog and his master found her; otherwise she would surely have died. She was carried down the mountain on an old enamelled sign that advertised Buckley's beer and woke in an itchy flannel nightgown that stank of old sweat. The farmer's wife was smearing some rancid, foul-smelling, grease on her chest and throat. She was in a fever for six days remembering little except for a dreamlike procession of different visitors, a doctor, a nurse, a few small children, the farmer's wife, the farmer himself and his dog, and the young wounded man with the pure singing voice. On the seventh day he came to see her and brought his mother and three sisters. They congratulated her and held her hand and kissed her. He spoke of their engagement and lifted her left hand to show off the gold and diamond ring she now wore. He had got the ring in France but failed to mention who he had bought it off or the dead hand it had been taken from.

As she lay there alone and exhausted she felt everything was drifting away from her; the water glass with its beaded linen cover, the walls of the room, the train that should have carried her to London, the boat to Calais, the Eiffel tower, Venice with its canals and gondolas, the Coliseum in Rome, the Parthenon, the Aegean sea, the olive groves, the brightly painted fishing boats, the dusty narrow streets that led to open squares with sparkling fountains. All were picture postcards blown out of her hands before she had a chance to send them.

Her marriage to a young Welsh war hero delighted everyone. She was back where she belonged. After the war it was the happy ending they had longed for. To go back on her word, to break her engagement was out of the question.

She married him, hoping for the best, but came to suffer him just as a soldier must suffer his wounds long after the battle had ended. Long after the wound was inflicted.

Dorothy's Journal
The Loire Valley, August 1958

Crossing the bridge our eyes were filled by the imposing presence of the chateau. Its towers and spires circled and chased by a murder of crows that swooped and cawed. I stopped to take a photograph while Thomas walked on, slowing his pace in deference to my dawdling ways. The weather which had promised fair when we drove towards the town now seemed on the brink of change. While one half of the sky was still blue and filled with high white clouds like those a child would draw, behind the chateau, a great mass seemed to gather and brew, deep lilac grey and gun-metal blue. Heavy and ominous.

Perfect for a moody shot of the thirteenth-century edifice,

with the black pen strokes of the winged birds adding drama and interest to the scene.

I took several shots and adjusted the metering to be sure of a good exposure. Thomas was now twenty paces ahead of me and had walked into the shot. He wore his black gabardine coat and dark moleskin trousers and leaned, as he always did, to the right, his cane taking the weight of his body as he limped slowly forward. With his dark head turned towards the chateau only his bony wrist and strong hand showed white. I took another shot, this one including him in the composition, but this was no cheery familial snapshot such as a wife should take of her husband, him smiling at the camera with some tourist destination serving as backdrop and proof of their trip, but one which rendered him an ominous stranger, a black-clad cripple; priest, sinner or necromancer. Perfecting the graphic composition as art-fully as if it had been sketched by Beardsley or Dore or Peake.

I had loaded the camera with a roll of 36 exposures and the dial showed 14 frames remained, but when I advanced the film it jammed. I increased the pressure with my thumb, but it did not give way. I knew I dare not force it as the film might snap.

'Come on, Dodo! It's going to rain,' Thomas called and as he did I felt the first few drops of rain. One splashed on my hand. Warmish rain that my skin was almost insensible to. I closed the camera's leather case and keeping the strap around my neck tucked it under my raincoat, then holding it securely between my hand and my body began to run after Thomas.

By the time I caught up with him the rain was torrential, Thomas's hair was plastered to his head, and his glasses were washed by a moving film of water. We were still a good distance from the entrance to the chateau and the winding road that led steeply up to it was lined with small houses of differing age, but there was no shop or cafe where we might seek shelter.

'Damn it!' Thomas shouted, but I barely heard him so loud, so all-consuming was the relentless pounding of the rain. The cobbled street had become a river and we seemed to wade through it as if for the sport of it. In this state, our shoes sodden and waterlogged, our clothes and hair drenched, everything wet through, there would be no chateau visit, no pleasant lunch on the square, nothing but a miserable retracing of our steps, a return to the small hotel and an afternoon amongst our dripping, steaming clothes and towels.

I was a few paces ahead of him and running blindly with my head bent forward, when a door to my left was abruptly pulled open and a beckoning arm urgently drew me in. I all but fell into the doorway and seconds later Thomas plunged in behind me, bumping against me and making me stagger forward into the room. I heard the door slam shut and then the noise of the storm was muted. It still lashed angrily against the window panes and roof, but it was powerless, a watery demon disarmed.

I sighed with relief and wiped my hand over my face and back over my hair, stemming the tide of liquid that ran down my forehead, into my eyes and poured off my nose and chin. It was only then that I took in the kind stranger who had opened her home to us. She was a tiny, ancient woman with fine white hair scraped back over a bony skull. Her back was hunched and her once ample bosom had sunk to a broad fleshy mound. She wore a shapeless frock that, because of her diminutive size, almost covered her ankles. Her surprising large feet had been pushed into a pair of worn sabots and grey lisle stockings drooped in rolls around her lower legs.

'Merci Madame! Merci!' Thomas said rapidly and with great warmth. She did not reply but nodded and gestured towards the old-fashioned black stove that dominated the room. She opened the iron door and poked at the coals, rousing them into fierce life, then turned her attention to me and partly by gesturing and partly tugging at one sleeve she encouraged me to take off my coat. There was a wooden airing rack over the stove and she unwound a rope to lower this, then draped my coat and Thomas's over it. Next she pointed at our shoes and from a copper box produced sheets of newspaper which she pushed into our shoes before lining them up on the hearth.

I took my camera from my neck and finding that it was still dry I put it on the large table by the side of the fire.

Our socks and stockings were taken and wrung out over the hearth to sizzle and steam, then they too were draped over the airing rack.

Thomas let out a steady stream of thanks and elaborately formal expressions of flattery and gratitude in perfect though badly accented French. He was in the middle of such a speech when our host began to shoo him away from the fire and towards a very narrow and steep flight of wooden stairs. Up he limped, his naked feet almost soundless on the steps, while his walking stick played a slow tattoo, one, then one, then one. She followed and I heard the floorboards creak overhead, then a door bang shut and the shuffle and slap of shoes as the old woman descended to turn her attentions to me. I was likewise shooed into another room. I understood at once that this was the old woman's bedchamber as there was a metal bedstead painted white and beside it a sturdy three-legged stool by which means she must have climbed in and out, for the bed was very high and she was remarkably small. Shrunk by old age and bent by osteoporosis, she was the size of a child of nine or ten. Once more she tugged at my clothes encouraging me to remove them. She was right of course; they were soaked quite through even down to my underwear. While I peeled off my cardigan and blouse, she searched in a tall chiffonier until she found garments she deemed suitable for me and draped these over the bed. As I stood there naked except for my brassiere and pants, her parting shot was to press a threadbare towel into my hands, then to mime, quite unnecessarily, the vigorous rubbing and tousling movements I should make to dry myself.

I suppose I might have found her manner overbearing, for she did not smile, nor show any expression of warmth, but gratitude and her great age combined with her almost doll-like size quite disarmed me. It was as if Thomas and I were two orphans of the storm she had chosen to take under her wing. Or two stray dogs, one of them lame and almost blind, that she had found cowering and half-starved in the street.

I wriggled out of my underwear, then rubbed myself dry and wrapped the towel around my head in a turban. I looked at the clothes she'd laid out for me, eggshell blue cami-knickers and a matching suspender belt made from silk with a trim of white lace, seamed stockings and black satin shoes with an ankle strap. Finally there was a lavender-grey dress of crepe de chine that fell from the shoulders to the waistband in soft folds, while the skirt, as it had been

125

cut on the bias, skimmed over the hips and fell in flowing airy flutes to just above the knee.

They were none of them garments I would have chosen to put on, being given more to practical skirts or slacks, to cotton blouses and aertex shirts, but once I had them on I could not help but examine my reflection in the looking glass. My skin, it seemed, had done well by its dowsing with rain water and looked soft and translucent. The dress was a very good fit, indeed it might have been made for me.

I rubbed my hair and found that the rain had brought out both the natural wave and a new glossy sheen. If I had ever wished for such a transformation or attempted one I never, in my wildest dreams, could have imagined the creature who now stood before me. I was (and perhaps it was the dim but electrified light that crept through the shutters, the antique glass in the mirror, the curious and transformative strangeness of the day's events) quite beautiful.

I gathered my wet things from the floor and went back into the room where the stove was. There was no sign of either Thomas or the old woman, so I busied myself by hanging my clothes on the rack, then when that was done I began to look with interest at the room itself and all it contained. Like many of the houses near the chateau this one was of a great age and the room was low ceilinged with roughly hewn smoke-darkened beams that here and there showed the wooden pegs used to drive them together and the marks of the tools that had made them. A great cauldron hung on a chain near the fire and the rafters were here and there festooned with bunches of drying herbs: bay and rosemary and lavender. In one corner a brownish side of bacon hung from a sharp hook and nearby some other object, black and crusted with age, also hung, though whether it was a truffle or dead mouse I could not tell. I only hoped that we would not be invited to eat it.

On the table next to my camera, there was a cracked earthenware bowl containing three hens' eggs. Beside it on a newspaper were six yellow tomatoes and a small cucumber with a skin as warty as a toad's. Then there was a bread board, a long knife with a striated bone handle and the heel of a baguette.

The floor was tiled in deep red and dipped in shallow troughs where many generations of feet had worn it down.

It seemed that time had stood still in this house for three perhaps four centuries. I looked ruefully at my camera and willed it not to be broken, then as there was still no sign of either Thomas or the old woman, I drew up one of the chairs, sat at the table and took the camera out of its case. I tried the lever to advance the film once more but it would not budge, then rather regretting the waste of unexposed film I pressed the button under the camera which released the locking mechanism and began to rewind the film onto the spool in the canister. If I was quick I could reload more film and get a few shots of this unique interior and, if I was allowed, a number of pictures of our ancient host too.

As a rule once the button is pressed the film winds easily and quickly back into the metal casing, but as I turned the knob I met with more and more resistance until I found I could not move it in either direction at all. Opening the back of the camera would mean ruining some or all of the frames I had taken that day. So unless I could find a dark-room, I would be without the camera for the rest of the trip. If it hadn't been for the frames I had taken of the chateau with the storm clouds behind and the circling crows and that last one when Thomas had stepped into the frame, I would have sacrificed the one roll of film for the sake of the many I planned to take.

I was agonising over my dilemma when I heard a step and then another on the stair. Slowly and irregularly at first, then they seemed to gather pace and gained the steady rhythm of one step after another, each the perfect echo of the one before and far too spritely, I thought, for either the old woman or Thomas.

The rain had begun to lose its intensity and now it stopped abruptly, making me as acutely aware of the swelling silence as if my ears had popped.

'Dodo?'

I turned and there was Thomas dressed more or less in the sort of clothes he usually wore, a white shirt, dark trousers, a jacket, but there was something distinctly different about them. The trousers were fuller and had pleats and turn ups, the jacket was far broader and also padded in the shoulder exaggerating his masculine form. His hair like mine seemed altered; it was combed back from the brow and shone as if he had dressed it with hair oil. But strangest of all was that he was standing up straight with his weight evenly distributed on both legs. He still held his cane but in such a way that it seemed a mere affectation, an accessory with no function besides its elegant silver tip and ivory handle.

'Where's the old dear?'

I shrugged.

'And what are you wearing? You look like a…'

I never discovered what I looked like to him at that moment, as the woman suddenly reappeared from the back room carrying a tray.

She fussed silently with three deep bowls, each of them

cracked and stained, putting them on the table and laying beside them mismatched soup spoons. From the oven she brought a small crock pot. It was glazed white and crudely painted in blue with rustic scenes that by the costumes of the shepherd and his maid must have been 18th century.

She beckoned us to the table and we sat, catching each other's eye as if to see if it was okay, if we should obey our host and eat with her. Thomas would have been all too aware of my American scruples in regard to hygiene. I tried to avoid looking too closely at the many chips and fissures in the crockery and did not let my mind dwell on the centuries of grime and fragments of food and germs they must contain.

She lifted the lid from the pot and inside we saw a thin yellowish broth, the steam carried to our nostrils a sweet garlicky smell. With a ladle she filled each of our bowls in turn. Thin strands of vermicelli slopped like white worms into the bowls and tiny green flecks floated on the oily surface.

'*Bon appetite!*' cried Thomas, all false conviviality, then he raised his spoon to his open mouth, clacking the metal against his teeth. The old woman picked up her bowl in both hands and held it by her gnarled fingertips as a diamond is held by the ring's claws.

'Goddamnit,' I thought, narrowing my eyes at my husband. 'I'll show you,' and I picked up my bowl, turning it in my fingers so that my lips should not come into direct contact with any of the cracks and I drank. Oh yes, I drank noisily and heartily and the old woman nodded at me in encouragement and ladled more soup into my bowl. I tipped my head back and let the fine threads of pasta slither into my mouth.

You can keep your Nathan's Hot Dogs. Your New York Strip, your Southern Chowder, I thought, I will eat only this. In this simple kitchen. Cooked by Mama.

I looked up and saw that Thomas was staring at me. He had stopped eating and laid aside his spoon. Defiantly I drank the last dregs, put down my bowl and, aware that a film of grease coated my mouth and chin, I drew the back of my hand over it, wiping it clean.

The light in the room suddenly changed, a warm golden glow spreading from the windows and across the floor, making the old woman's face lose its dull grey pallor. Her cheeks seemed fuller, pinker and though still lined by age, she seemed to shed many weary years. She smiled indulgently at me and I melted under her benevolent gaze, held fixedly in her twinkling grey-blue eyes.

Thomas stood up abruptly and began removing his clothes from the drying rack. His cane, I noticed, was abandoned, hooked over the back of his chair. I wondered why he had ever bothered with it; his injured leg had healed long ago.

'They're just about dry,' he said. 'And the sun's come out!'

He made two roughly folded piles of clothing and brought mine to me at the table. I shook my head and barely glanced at them. Angrily he put them on the table, the plain white cotton undergarments uppermost. They were like something a child would wear and I was no longer a child.

'Dodo,' he said. 'It's time we left!'

I looked up at him; he'd run his hand through his hair so that it no longer lay flat and glossy but fell in a short dry-looking fringe over his forehead. He looks like a foreigner, I thought, like one of those tommy boys from England or worse, those doughboy Yanks.

He rolled his eyes then gathered up his clothes and stomped up the stairs. I listened to the creak of the floorboards overhead, the sounds were interspersed with other noises, the regular tick, tick, tick of the mantle clock, the muted crack and whispered collapse of the coals shifting in the fire.

I sighed and smiled happily at Mama. It was good to be home. She went to the cupboard in the wall by the stove and brought out two small glasses and the bottle of *eaux-de-vie*. She filled the glasses to the brim and we each dipped our heads to take the first sip before the drink was lifted to the lips.

I gave a little shudder at the first swallow as I had always done as a young girl. I closed my eyes and sat back in the chair, running my tongue over my lips savouring the fiery sweetness of the digestif. It was pleasantly warm in the room and peaceful. I dozed off for a couple of minutes, no more, and dreamt that I was a bird. I didn't know what sort of bird I was, but I was soaring on a thermal with my wings outstretched, my feathers stirring and fluttering in the wind. I seemed to have no weight, it was effortless and it was happiness such as I had never known before.

I did not ever wish to leave that dream, but a hand was shaking me awake and there was Thomas, dressed in his own clothes again.

The old woman had moved to an armchair by the fire where she slept, her mouth hanging open slightly, her chin sagging on her chest.

Thomas led me to the door, tugging gently at my hand as I gazed at the old woman and hung back like a recalcitrant child. Then we were outside on the street once more and

Thomas slammed the door behind us decisively.

'You look ridiculous, you know,' he said in a hiss. 'Here are your things.' He pushed a brown paper parcel into my arms. 'It goes without saying that you have shocked me. How could you drink that dishwater she served us? I thought you'd have the good sense to pretend like I did. And as for that liquor! My god, you're quite drunk, aren't you?'

He set off up the steep hill towards the entrance to the chateau. He was carrying his cane tucked under one arm and striding ahead. I ran a few paces to catch up with him, but my head was reeling, and the shoes I wore might have done justice to walking, but running uphill half drunk in the blazing heat and light of mid-afternoon?

A small truck came rattling round the bend and I saw the driver's eye follow me, turning his head to pucker his lips as he let out a shrill whistle of approval.

Thomas had rounded the bend and by the time I caught up he was entering the carved archway that led into the chateau. I followed and found myself at the foot of a broad spiral staircase. I paused a moment listening to distant echoing steps going up, further and further away from me. I must have gone up forty or so steps, when I stopped, opened the package, retrieved my walking shoes and slipped them on. My head was clearing; I felt energised and so I began to move faster. The dress brushed against my legs and the rubber-soled shoes gave grace and accuracy to my fast-moving feet. Up and up I went, stopping once to gaze out of a narrow window down at the cobbled courtyard far below, where other visitors milled about in pairs and groups. One man stood just below me, a camera aimed upwards, obscuring his face. Where was my camera?

Thomas had dragged me away so suddenly I had not even thought of it. I threw myself at the stairs again, running, taking two, then three steps at a time. Surely he would have picked the camera up for me. It had been there on the table near his elbow. He knew what it meant to me!

I reached the top of the stairs. They ended in a circular well in which there was only one door. A wooden door that was banded with black iron and scarred all over from bottom to top with carved signatures, many of which were dated. I saw the year 1668 swing away from my gaze as I pushed the door open. A clear fresh wind hit me, tossing my hair and rippling through my dress. Ahead of me was a narrow walkway that led from one tower to the next. On one side was a crenellated wall, on the other side nothing but a sheer drop. Thomas stood halfway, he had the camera in his hands and was leaning forward slightly from the waist aiming the lens at the courtyard. I watched him for a moment with relief, thankful that he had remembered the camera. Then I realised that any shots he took would ruin my pictures by producing double exposures.

'Thomas!' I called. 'Don't!'

He turned sharply at the sound of my voice and his walking stick, which he had tucked under his arm, clattered onto the walkway, then half rolled, half bounced off the path. He lunged sideways, his hand clawing helplessly for the cane, then his injured leg buckled and, both arms flailing, he pitched forward over the edge.

There was nothing slow or magnificent about his descent, it was nothing like flying. When he landed there was a noise that I will never forget. A woman screamed, but it seemed very far away. I don't think it was me.

I stood there blinking for a moment, hardly believing

what had happened. I could not take it in. I stared at the place where he had stood as if willing what I saw to develop fully just as I watched images appear in the developing fluid in the darkroom. Then my eyes went to the ground where his feet had been. There was my camera, the case half open, the neck strap making a looped whorl. It had landed on its back, the delicate glass lens uppermost. Unbroken.

MRS DUNDRIDGE

Mrs Dundridge was extravagant with boiling water. She bathed every day.

Her neighbours often commented on it. They saw her from their windows lugging the heavy tin bath up the steps to her back garden and tipping the milky water onto the lawn. The water from their own tin baths was grey, almost black sometimes.

And the things she hung on her washing line? Scraps of flesh-coloured satin, pale blue chemises, white leg-shaped stockings kicking about like girls in a burlesque show. She'd catch her death dressing like that. Where were the sensible white lisle vests, the fleecy liberty bodices, the voluminous bloomers, the knitted wool stockings?

She'd not got an ounce of spare flesh on her either, and that couldn't be good.

The neighbours all knew her story, how her young husband, a miner, had joined the Royal Engineers at the first call. He was one of those who marched away cheerfully while the brass band played.

Mind you, he'd been at that pit that had a fall in 1920, so chances were he'd be done for either way. Though if he'd stayed perhaps he'd have given her some babies, then she wouldn't be so alone, would she?

Ah, poor thing.

She was universally pitied for the tragedy of her life, as much as she was scorned. She lacked good sense.

You'd think she'd go back to her people. Someone said she had a sister in England. Bristol wasn't it? A place called Coalpit Heath. Must have been mines there too. But not such a limitless coal stream as the one hidden under the hills and valleys of South Wales. Black gold.

Poor dab. Some people say she's waiting for him to come back, that's why she won't leave.

Mr Clements paid her court. Think of that. With all his money and that nice house on the hill. Everyone knows Mr Clements as he does his rounds once a week collecting money for the funeral plan. In the window of his shop he's got a clock and a little sign that says 'It's never too soon'. The clock keeps good time though, but you can barely look at it without remembering that death is waiting for each of us. Well, not everyone would want to marry an undertaker. Not her, anyway, not for all the tea in China.

Hardly anyone's been in that house of hers. She keeps you on the doorstep. Locks her doors, back and front, even when she's at home.

Oh, she must get lonely, though.

Mrs Davies the dressmaker knew her best. But Mrs Dundridge always went to her, not the other way round. Always paid up front. Never a quibble about the price. Took Mrs Davies pictures torn from fancy magazines, said, 'I'd like this one made up in violet crepe, but with three-quarter sleeves and no bow at the front.'

But Mrs Dundridge was good to her. Mrs Davies' husband was gone too. Lost at sea with the merchant navy. And her with six boys and no war pension. As soon as the eldest, Gerald, could, Mrs Dundridge had given him little jobs around the house; you'd see him carrying sacks of spuds, or up a ladder fishing leaves out of the guttering.

Good as gold that boy was. And handsome!

Oh you'd think he was Valentino. And clever too, went to the Grammar School. Could have gone to University, but wouldn't leave his mother. Works in the bank now. Oh you should see his hands, lovely they are, clean nails and everything.

If it hadn't been for Mrs Dundridge and her fancy Paris fashions that boy would've gone down the pit. Or off to sea like his father.

But there was something odd about her though. Something not right.

Poor dab.

Mrs Dundridge put the big pan of water on the copper and while she waited for it to boil, she turned the pages of her *Ladies Home Journal*. There was an article about the joys of modern indoor plumbing, accompanied by photos of a gleaming white bath with hot and cold taps, and crisp black and white checkerboard tiles on the walls, and marble-effect lino on the floor. The height of luxury. But the article, when it got down to the nitty gritty, was full of assumptions about the reader; namely that the lady of the house lived in London – or its sprawling suburbs at the very least. At the end of the article the lady was furnished with details of recommended suppliers; Harrods was listed first, then others in Fulham, Ealing, Hampstead, Windsor, Hove, Reading, Guildford, Chelsea and so on. The only one mentioned outside the closed circle of the Home Counties was in Edinburgh.

A proper indoor bathroom would be nice. There's no harm in dreaming. But it was warm by the fire in the back parlour, and she's careful about splashes, and put the oilskin cloth under the bath before she filled it. Why, she even had music to listen to while she soaked, timing her baths to coincide with the broadcast from the Wigmore Hall on the BBC. Three drops of lavender oil to soften and scent the water, a towel warming on the fireguard. She luxuriated. It couldn't be such a sin, could it? Cleanliness was next to Godliness after all. Mrs Dundridge had her own ideas about God, too.

She believed in God, but not a vengeful god. Her God, were He to look inside her heart, would see that there was not a shred of anything bad within. Nothing evil anyway. But other people would see her differently. Especially if they knew about Gerald Davies.

The pan was boiling, so she extinguished the flame under the copper, and using a cloth to grip the hot handle and another to heft and steady the base of the pot, she carefully poured the water into the tin bath and added the lavender oil. Moist scented air filled the room pleasantly. She had already pulled the curtains shut. They only looked out onto a path by the side of the house and the neighbour's high brick wall, but one had to be careful.

Leaving the water to cool, and taking the back door key with her, she went out to the privy, which was thankfully only six steps away from the kitchen. Some people had them at the bottom of the garden and you'd see people hurrying down their garden paths in their nightclothes with old newspaper in one hand and perhaps a full chamber pot in the other.

She locked her back door from the outside, even though where she was going was only a few feet away, and it was a peaceful Sunday evening and at seven-thirty, still light.

Her imagination, the same imagination that shaped God to her own design, was relentless; it sent swarthy feet tip-

138

toeing past the wooden door of the privy, it made heavy hands with dirty fingers stealthily open her back door, it put shadowy men behind the couch in the best room, in the cupboard under the stairs, in the wardrobe.

So she locked the back door, locked herself in the privy, sat there gripping the key in her hand, alert to any sound or movement in the small yard beyond.

Gerald had promised to come to see her that night. Her feelings towards him were curiously mixed; lately he had grown so tall and manly that she often thought of him as a sort of father figure, but there again she vividly remembered him as a young boy of fifteen with only a slight dark fuzz on his upper lip and a wiry long body that had yet to develop the muscles and chest hair and broad shoulders of the man he would become. Back then she had felt worldly and maternal, like a teacher who would guide him towards the exquisite experience of love between a man and a woman. He had been dutiful in his lessons, had practised his techniques on her body like a virtuoso musician doing scales on a grand piano. But now she sensed that she was losing him.

Oh, and she had always known that one day she would. That he would go off into the world and find some pretty young virgin to love and marry. What she hadn't anticipated was the sense of loss she felt, the anger and resentment at the insult to her.

And when he was sixteen he had (silly boy) told her he loved her, swore he would always love her and asked her to marry him. He'd even bought a ring from Woolworth's; she'd worn it on the third finger of her right hand, until it turned her skin green and the claws that held the glass diamond bent and broke, disgorging the fake gemstone and rendering the ring an ugly spiteful weapon that snagged stockings, satin and skin.

He'd been spending a lot of his time with the ironmonger's daughter. What was her name? It was hard to distinguish these young women; they all seemed to dress the same, to tie their hair in girlish braids or ponytails, and to hare around in packs giggling wildly. Edna. That was it. Edna Thomas.

There was a rumour that Gerald and Edna were courting, but until she heard it from his own lips she wouldn't believe it.

Naked, she eased herself into the tub. She washed hurriedly, soaping under her arms, between her toes and behind her ears, before using a flannel to wash between her legs. She was careful to rinse all the soap from the soft black hair that grew there in such remarkable abundance.

After her bath Mrs Dundridge dressed in a new frock, it was made from a glazed cotton fabric with white flowers on a dark blue ground. It suited her figure, emphasized her small waist and slim legs.

Gerald arrived before she had a chance to put on her shoes or stockings. His knock at the door; two sharp taps, then three longer ones, sent a quiver of butterflies through her stomach where they trembled and thrilled in a delicious ripple of anticipation.

She hurried to unlock the door, and then airily, coldly – like the mistress of the house instructing a servant of the lowest order – she waved him in.

He shut the door and had only stepped forward two paces when she threw her arms around his neck and showered him with hot lavender-scented kisses.

It had not always been like this; she used to be shy and

reluctant, would move around him or sit close to him, accidentally grazing her body against his. The moth and the candle; his young heat, her willful proximity. He had been young and naive at the beginning, and she had been subtle. She had not seemed to notice how he watched her, nor that she'd accidentally left two buttons on a blouse undone. She seemed oblivious when she leaned across the table to pour his tea and he could see the inviting valley between her swelling breasts.

His mother had taught him to feel both pity and gratitude for this childless widow. Mrs Dundridge had helped their family by giving Mrs Davies well-paid work, and she had extended her generosity by employing the eldest son too.

'She might take a shine to you,' Gerald's mother had said, 'and remember she has no children of her own.'

Mrs Davies had an idea that the widow would become so fond of Gerald that she might name him in her will. She pictured Gerald inheriting Mrs Dundridge's house. She pictured Mrs Dundridge in an oak casket dead of consumption at a tragically young age. Mrs Davies would of course make her the most beautiful shroud. She imagined an open casket, a white satin dress, delicately hand-stitched and embroidered with seed pearls.

Gerald stood awkwardly by the coat stand in the hall, Mrs Dundridge had caught him off balance and he rested one hand on the wall to steady himself as she ran her tongue over his neck and hissed in his ear, 'Oh Gerald, my god, Gerald.'

She tugged at his shirttails, pulling them and his vest out of his trousers so that she could run her hands over the bare skin of his back.

'Darling,' he said, meaning to arrest this intense assault,

but she found his mouth and pushed her tongue into it. Thus silenced he found his body responding even as his mind resisted.

Mrs Dundridge felt dizzy and, as sometimes happened lately, she could sense an odd squeaky pulse as blood pumped through a vein at the base of her skull. She wanted Gerald to lift her in his arms and carry her upstairs and force her onto the bed. She would have liked to say, 'No, no, please. Don't, it's wrong,' but the one time she had said that he had actually stopped what he was doing and apologised. She wanted him to want her with all the swirling energy with which she wanted him.

As it had been at the beginning.

Suddenly, in the middle of that achingly beautiful kiss, he turned his head and moved his body up and away like a diver exploding out of the water and into the air. 'Listen,' he said. His mouth was cloying and tacky, 'Could I have a glass of water?'

'Oh, are you alright?' Mrs Dundridge asked. The skin around her mouth was pink and raw-looking he noticed. His doing as he hadn't shaved since the morning before.

Together they went through the house to the back parlour, where he dispensed with the civilities of the proffered glass, and bent his head under the tap to drink noisily from the cold torrent.

He sat at the table and asked if there was anything to eat. She offered to fry him some bacon and eggs, or to open a tin of salmon, but he said that bread was all he wanted.

She stood by the table a few feet away from him, her body set squarely towards him and with the bread loaf under one arm she sawed away with the serrated knife to produce a thin slither of bread. This was typical of her refinement; the daintiness of everything – there would be no doorstops of bread and dripping under her roof.

He wanted to snatch the bread and the knife from her and stuff his whole hand into the loaf, pull out the soft centre just as if he was cleaning the entrails from a rabbit, to jam it into his mouth and eat without any concession to good manners.

But he didn't, he just watched as she first buttered, then sawed off each slice. Sometimes they were so wafer thin that it seemed it was only the salty, bright yellow butter that held each slice together.

The redness had faded from around her mouth, but now her cheeks wore high spots of colour. He still resented the way she had rejected his wedding proposal when he was sixteen. Resented it, even as he had grown to realise how preposterous it was, how much of an escape he had had. He'd noticed lately how her hair had developed strands of silvery white, how her cheeks often seemed sunken and drawn, how her eyelids were weighted and creased and the eyes themselves did not shine with the same clarity as before.

'I'm going away tomorrow,' he said at last.

She had laid each buttered slice of bread on a white dinner plate, stacking them up edge to edge.

'I've got some cheese on the cold shelf. Or ham?'

'I'll be gone for a few days.'

She continued to slice the bread, sawing it inwards towards her pale chest and the softly swelling breasts, and the heart that lay hidden beneath.

He found himself picturing her heart, big as an ox's and liver-coloured, throbbing with the same rhythm as a vein in his temple.

'I don't want anymore,' he said, meaning the bread and

butter.

She understood. There was no difficulty whatsoever. She put the kitchen knife down on the table and stood the flat heel of the loaf beside it. On the white plate the stack of sliced bread lay untouched.

He noticed how the bread in its neat stack on the plate mimicked the uncut half loaf; they were the same shape and approximately the same height. It reminded him of a trick he knew; you took an unpeeled banana, and with a needle and thread it was possible to slice the soft fruit inside, so that when you gave the banana to an unwitting person they would be amazed to see it fall apart in neat pieces.

Mrs Dundridge felt broken inside. She saw that she had been foolish; being older, wiser she should have known better. She had not known that love would slowly ambush her.

But there was no difficulty whatsoever. She showed no outward sign of anger or pain, but busied herself around the room.

This is why women have kitchens, they can mortify their hands with scalding water and carbolic soap, cut themselves with sharp knives, sweat themselves in the sauna of a summer Sunday dinner, make thunderous music with their pots and pans.

Saying nothing, Mrs Dundridge got a sheet of greaseproof paper from the drawer, laid the stack of bread and butter on top, then folded it into a neat package. Gerald watched her hands, but avoided her eyes. She pushed the wrapped bread towards him; he might have been her husband then, taking sandwiches to eat down the mine, or her child going off to school.

'Go,' she said.

And willingly he did as he was ordered.

RITUAL, 1969

The lesson began. The teacher, a woman of around forty, with stiffly styled hair that was a gaudy yellow-blonde, cut in a sort of long bob, wore one heavy copper pendant necklace and another longer one that seemed to have been made out of varnished slices of banana.

'Now children, today we are going to read a poem called The Moon and the Yew Tree.'

Mimeographed copies of the poem were distributed among the thirty or so thirteen year olds.

'The Moon and the Yew Tree,' the teacher declaimed, about to begin her recitation of the poem, but then struck by an idea, she hesitated, and almost as an aside, added, 'Now who can tell me something about yew trees?'

She was expectant, confidently anticipating a number of eager hands to shoot up. When the children's response was only a little mild shuffling, interspersed by the odd turn of a head to see if any other member of the class had raised a hand, the teacher looked a little ruffled. Composing herself, she decided that perhaps her question had been too broad. She tried again.

'Well then, who can tell me where yew trees are grown?'

As in geography class, one child might have taken a wild stab at China or Scotland or Egypt, but none did.

'Come on, children, where are yew trees grown? Where do you always see yew trees?'

Silence. The children growing somewhat wide-eyed in

145

their shared astonishment to discover this black hole in the sum of their knowledge.

'Yew trees. Think!' The last word drawn out, an order, a prayer. 'Where do you find yew trees?'

More silence. No child even prepared to make a guess.

'One of you must know. Don't be shy. If you know put your hand up.'

This ploy also fails. Shyness and its sister, modesty, are not staying the children's hands. The truth is no one knows. No one has a clue. No one remembers the biology lesson about yew trees, nor the geography lesson (though they do know where cocoa and rubber trees come from), nor religious studies with its talking trees and burning bushes. They know oak trees by their wavy leaves, holly by its prickly ones, Christmas trees which are pointy and pine-scented. Willows that weep to make secret cave-like hiding places. Chestnut trees by the shape of their large leaves, their sticky buds and glorious conkers. But yew trees? A blank. A blank in a forest of vaguely known and unknown trees. Elms. Monkey puzzle trees. Some lose their leaves in the autumn, some don't. Evergreen trees. Trees with beautiful deep red leaves. Tall firs with fallen cones at the base which can be used to tell the weather – open in fair weather, closed for the rain.

The teacher paces at the front of the class. She is incredulous. The children's eyes follow her. She wears a long sleeveless cardigan made from crocheted squares of brightly coloured wool; orange, green, turquoise and purple. A tan-coloured suede skirt with poppers up the front. A yellow polo-neck jumper. Purple wool tights. Brown boots. The children, except for their white shirts, are uniformly grey like baby birds.

'Do you mean to tell me,' she says, 'that not one of you.

146

Not one, knows where yew trees grow!'

Somehow the poem itself has been forgotten. The yew tree, the damnable yew tree stands in the way blocking even the moon. Nothing can get past it. Most notably the teacher.

'In all my years I have never been so shocked. Does no one really have any idea? I cannot believe it. I really can't! Yew trees!'

To be certain the issue isn't deafness, she picks up a chalk and with strident, noisy, dust-making jabs she writes on the blackboard, YEW TREES.

Then once more, chin now jutting, she scans every upturned face to find what look like expressions of beguiling innocence. Or as is more likely the case, a generation of dull, blank stupidity, each child culpable, wantonly incurious, glazed over by cheap sweets and that babbling monster of nonsense, the TV.

She paces, seemingly muttering to herself, though still loud enough for every child's edification. 'This is common knowledge. This is something everyone knows. This is hardly obscure or arcane. This is everywhere. You open your eyes. There it is. I'm sure I knew this when I was five years old! Perhaps when I was younger. I can't believe that none of you know this. Some of you must! What is it then? You're not shy, none of you. You're not stupid. Oh, no, I don't believe that! So then is it me? Is it poetry? Have none of you ever been touched by words? Have your senses not thrilled at the recognition of something better than *She Loves You, Yeah, Yeah, Yeah or Hey Diddle Diddle?* Or those awful advert jingles for Turkish Delight and Pepsodent and hands that do dishes and don't forget the fruit gums.'

She stops pacing, closes her mouth, breathes in and out

deeply through her nose. Her chest rises and falls. Her neck-laces shift and chime against one another.

Time itself is held in check by the yew tree. The lesson does not progress, but turns around and around on this one subject – a solitary tree pitched into blackness by its obscurity.

'Think of where the dead are buried,' she says. 'What do we call those places?'

At last several hands shoot into the air. The teacher picks one, nodding enthusiastically at the boy in the third row whose fair hair looks faintly greenish in the fluorescent light.

'A graveyard, Miss.'

'Very good,' she says. Then directly addressing him, she adds, 'And what sort of trees do we always see in grave-yards?'

He frowns, puzzling over this. In his mind he is roaming the churchyard where his nan is buried. He sees gravestones, some flat and rectangular like platforms, others that are simple grey tablets with arched tops, some are tall obelisks, and lastly there are three stone angels, one of which seems to cry grey tears. There are flowers in metal containers, some brown and wilting, others new and bright. What else? Grass, a few weeds. And trees, indistinct at the edges of his vision. Then there! There in the corner, near the red brick wall that flanks the pavement, he seems to see a lush, berry-covered holly bush, as broad as it is tall.

'Holly trees?' he says.

'No!' the teacher roars. 'For goodness' sake. Not holly trees. We are not talking about holly trees!'

Another child puts up her hand.

'At last,' the teacher thinks. 'Finally.'

'Yes, Janet?' she says, eyes narrowing, a grin smearing itself over her apricot-lipsticked mouth and long nicotine teeth.

'In the church we go to there is a holly tree, because at Christmas, the Sunday school get to cut some to take home.'

Little noises of assent run like the rumour of revolution around the class.

'Some graveyards might have holly trees,' the teacher says heavily emphasising the first word. 'But…' She stops speaking, walks around her desk, sits down and with elbows resting on its top, cradles her head in both hands, looking to the children as if she were about to cry.

They exchange quick glances with one another, frown, shrug their shoulders, shake their heads.

The room they are in is on the top floor of a huge school that was built only two years before in the brutalist style. The classrooms are on three floors, divided by dimly lit corridors that pass down the centre like the black veins in shrimps' bodies, door after door after door leading off. In other buildings there are a swimming pool, a gymnasium, changing rooms, an assembly hall.

The children are always told how lucky they are to have this wonderful school with its many playgrounds and sports fields, its light and airy classrooms, its specially designed facilities for teaching cookery and metal and woodwork, the physics, chemistry, biology and language labs. Its dedicated, learned and enthusiastic staff. The teachers are a diverse bunch; some are young and energetic, others are of a middling age, a few are old and lame, warty and peculiar. Some of the male teachers fought in the war. Some inspire fear, a very few inspire love, some are openly challenged, but none are ever pitied. All are sanctioned to use physical

149

violence; most of them are capable of lashing out suddenly with hands, or rulers or wooden board dusters.

There are 1,500 children in this school and of the thirty in this English class none know a single thing of any significance about yew trees.

The school has been built on top of a hill in the centre of a housing estate. In winter there is nothing to buffer the icy wind that comes scouring over the playing fields and black tarmac netball courts. Nothing to protect the girls' legs in their knee-high white socks, yet there they are; shivering though each break and lunch hour. Breathing in the yellow stink of sulphur when the wind comes from the industrial east.

In milder weather these girls perform their ancient game of levitation, not knowing where it has come from; nor that it was first mentioned by the diarist, Pepys in 1665.

She looks ill, she is ill, she looks dead, she is dead.

One girl lies down on a low wall, five others surround her. They must not giggle, must not break the spell. When the chanting voices have each repeated the spell, they lift the girl on high using just the tips of two fingers each.

They know about this, but they do not know yew trees.

The school bell rings upon the teacher's silence. The poem, its 'cold and planetary' secrets and its author (who gassed herself six years ago) are all eclipsed.

Quietly the children push back their chairs and, gathering their belongings, they file in silence from the room. The teacher does not look up until the last pupil has gone.

She opens her eyes to thirty empty chairs and desks. And on the desks thirty rectangles of paper, every word unread.

FALLEN APPLES

The old woman walked down to the bottom of the garden again. She gazed up at the apple tree and shook her head gently as if her old skull – almost empty now of memories – was moved by the slight breeze. The green apples that hung above her head were still tight and hard and small. They reminded her of something, but she couldn't think what. She moved away from the tree and walked towards the house again, then stopped.

Nancy watched the old woman from the bathroom window. Minutes before she had flung it wide open even though her sister Martha had said to keep it closed. Nancy had wrapped her wet hair up in a towel and wore only a bra and jeans. Her skin was damp and greasy with bath oil. It was too hot to keep the window tightly closed. Too hot to wear many clothes.

The old woman in the garden next door, Nancy thought, walked like an insect, there was something light and mechanical about her movements. Even the old woman herself looked puzzled about this, as if she could not understand why she walked in this strange way, with her legs and hands plucking at the air as if they had just been freed from gravity. She was tiny, and fleshless. The bones and veins showed through her hands in a way that reminded Nancy of an anatomical diagram.

The old woman looked at the house, upstairs at the window she saw a young girl with her hair in a towel looking down on her. She stopped walking and stared hard. It troubled her that she could not quite remember whom this person was that she was staring at. She had an uneasy sense that it was her younger self up there in the bathroom. She had done that one day surely – stood by the open window after her bath and then he had seen her from the garden and called up at her and asked her to stay where she was.

Except that she had been naked. He had run into the house to fetch his camera and she had waited obediently. Later he had asked her to remove the towel from her head and then he'd photographed her long wet hair as it clung in glossy waves to her freckled naked back. Then he had photographed her leaning over the sink with one knee bent slightly. But perhaps she wasn't remembering right, though she remembered the pictures of herself emerging in the white enamel dishes, the strange red light in the darkroom and the indelible smell of the chemicals.

The old woman and the girl stood in their respective places watching each other.

Now it occurred to her that perhaps the girl at the window was her mama. A very young version of her mama – which meant that she herself must be only six or seven years old. Had she done something naughty? She was suddenly very anxious about this. Would she be punished? Would Mama cry as she had cried after the glass vase made by the Frenchman was broken?

Nancy saw these changing emotions flicker over the old woman's face. It was like watching a TV screen with the

FALLEN APPLES

sound down and a bad signal. The old woman's hair was frazzled and grey and seemed to spring from her head like a halo of wire wool. Nancy had watched the old woman brushing it one day. Someone had put one of the dining chairs on the lawn under the washing line and the old woman had sat there in the pink quilted dressing gown she always wore, jerkily moving the brush over her head but not really making a good job of brushing it.

Martha had told her that there were no mirrors in the ground floor flat where the old woman lived – that the old woman had smashed all of them and wasn't allowed any more, but no one could explain why this was, except to say that mirrors frightened the woman.

If she were that old, Nancy thought, she would not want to see her reflection. She never wanted to grow old.

The old woman continued to gaze up at Nancy as if she were waiting for something. Nancy smiled and slowly raised her hand and moved it back and forth in an approximation of a wave. She wasn't even sure if the old woman could see her, but she wanted to be kind at that moment, to show that she was friendly.

The sky was pale china blue. It had rained in the night and the air had that steamy claustrophobic dampness about it that would burn off as the sun rose. At eleven o'clock Nancy was due to meet Sam near the old hospital. They would go for a walk – perhaps along the beach or through the park. They would walk holding hands and every now and then they would stop and kiss. Sam spoke with a soft low voice and a slight accent, he was twenty-three and Nancy had told him she was eighteen, when really she was still four months away from her sixteenth birthday. He'd told her he had come as a child from one of those Eastern

153

European countries whose name had now changed. There had been a war, but he would not talk about it. His parents had fled to the West and now he had fled his parents. He lived in his car mostly. Worked sometimes as a washer-up in hotels. The police were looking for him. Sometimes he stole things, but only just enough to get by. Nancy was in love. She had known him three days. She planned to run away with him. If he asked her to.

The old woman saw the girl at the window wave. Goodbye, she thought, goodbye. Must I go now? Should I wave at Mama even though I don't want to go to school and leave her?

Or perhaps the girl was not waving goodbye, but hello. She is waving hello because I've returned from somewhere – but where? And how long was I gone?

Or she is waving me away. Yes, that is it, I do not belong in this garden and yet I do not think I can climb the high brick wall to escape. I have been naughty and Mama will punish me.

Anxiety rose in the old woman. It was terrible, this sense of something wrong, something broken or lost. Her breath came in little sighed gasps - oh, oh, oh – much too quiet for the girl at the window to hear. The old woman found herself turning away from the house. It was time to go down to the apple tree again.

Nancy waited until the old woman had returned to the apple tree, then she pulled shut the frosted window and turned the latch. She removed the damp towel and threw back her head so that her wet hair landed with a cool slap on her naked back.

No make-up, not even mascara. No perfume or deodorant.

He had said he didn't like it. But she was afraid of smelling bad. Yesterday she had washed her armpits three times, once in the public toilets near the law courts, once in a pub toilet and once in the stream that ran through the wooded area of the park.

Sam talked a lot about philosophy and politics. Sometimes he reminded her of a priest, a kind of modern day visionary. Everything about the world was bad and wrong, he said. We have gone down the wrong path; we are lost.

She wished he would tell her about the war in his country, about his family fleeing. He had experienced at firsthand things she had only seen on the TV or in the papers. This gave his words and ideas gravitas. He peeled the world like an egg, sneered at it. Showed her that inside it was quite rotten. If he asked her, she would run away with him, would do anything for him.

The old woman looked up at the apples. Am I Eve? she thought.

Then she had one of those rare lucid memories. He had taken a photo of her as she sat at the polished table in the old dining room. She had to take her clothes off and sit with a pile of books on the chair so that her breasts were level with the table. He'd put a line of apples across the edge and her breasts were meant to join this parade of round green fruit. It was meant to look surreal, but neither he nor she had liked the photo in the end. I am trying too hard, he said, it should be natural, spontaneous.

The old woman repositioned her feet and reached up as if about to pluck one of the fruits from the tree. She turned towards the house and gazed at the long path that wove through the garden. She had expected to see him standing there, his head and shoulders hidden beneath the black hunched cloth, his eyes replaced by the silvery glint of the camera lens.

In a book someone had called her his muse. Mama said he'd turned her into a whore and then he'd disowned her.

But there was no one standing in the garden with her. The apples were too high to reach. She slowly lowered her arm and wondered what she was doing there. The apples were not ready to be picked. They were small and hard and sour. Had she done something wrong? She had not meant to.

Nancy told Martha she was going for a walk.

Again? Martha had said.

Nancy didn't answer. She'd taken a bottle of red wine from the rack in the dining room. She didn't care if Martha discovered this later, but didn't want her to find out now. She had meant to take the corkscrew too, but Martha was in the kitchen chopping onions so it was impossible. She hung around in the kitchen for a little while, hoping that Martha would go out to put washing on the line, or disappear upstairs to the bathroom. But all Martha did was chop onion after onion. For soup, probably. Nancy didn't like soup, especially not onion soup.

The old woman was still down by the apple tree. Nancy stared at her through the lace curtain that hung over the kitchen window. She did not pull the curtain to one side, but gazed directly through it liking the way it turned the world pale and hazy.

–What do you think she's doing down there? Nancy asked.

Martha glanced in the direction of the window; her eyes

were pink and streaming.

–Oh, I don't know. Why don't you ask her?

Nancy missed the note of sarcasm in Martha's voice.

–Really? Do you think I should?

–Yeah, said Martha. I'm sure it'll all make sense then.

–Oh, Nancy said, understanding the sarcasm at last; hating Martha for her bitter tongue. If Sam asked her, she would definitely run away with him. He'd talked about buying a van. They could live in a van.

–So, are you meeting someone? Martha asked. Having a rendezvous with a secret lover?

There it was – the nasty ironic tone again.

–Yeah, that's right and we're going to run away together and live in a van and have babies and love each other forever.

–Hah! Martha made a scoffing noise. Dream on.

Nancy scowled at Martha's back, mouthed a curse before turning again to the window. The old woman had raised her hand as if reaching for an apple, then held it there a moment before she turned to look towards the house. Expectation, then a look of puzzled disappointment passed over her face, followed by an expression of almost tangible sadness.

Maybe Nancy would ask her why she kept going down to the apple tree. Maybe the old woman was just waiting for someone to ask. Maybe she had a thousand stories to tell and no one to listen.

–I'm going now, Nancy said to Martha's back.

Martha did not speak, just shrugged her shoulders as if shaking something off.

Nancy had a sense that it would always be like this, that Martha would chop onions for eternity and the old woman would be stuck forever in that place under the apple tree. Nancy could go away for a hundred years and on her return it would still be like this.

Nancy picked up her bag; the weight of the filched wine bottle gave her great satisfaction. She slammed the front door hard on her way out. The loud noise had a pleasant angry finality about it. If she felt like it, if he asked her, she'd leave with him today, never go back.

The old woman looked up at the window where she had seen the young woman, but she wasn't there anymore. The old woman remembered her mother crying again.

-If you leave don't come back, she'd said.

But then she had come back and it was her mother who had gone.

And he was gone too, the man with the camera.

She looked at the apples hanging on the tree again. Still not ripe. But once again she pretended to reach for them. She held the pose for as long as she could although her arm was shaking slightly with the effort of it. She was waiting for the sound of the camera shutter that would release her from the spell.

She heard a distant thud and feeling a sense of relief she lowered her trembling arm, then turned smiling in the direction of the empty path.

He's hurried off to develop the glass plate, she thought, and remembered the darkroom – how the plain white paper was tilted to and fro in the clear liquid of the tray until the image began to emerge. At first you couldn't see what the picture was. Then the pale grey unreadable shadows gradually deepened until at last she saw herself as he had seen her – a creature who seemed to be both like and unlike herself.

She turned in the direction of the old house again and began walking towards it.

Behind her, the tree with its twisted branches and pale emerald leaves and unripe fruit stood as if waiting. Its shadow on the grass was as intricate and still as a photograph. A breeze shook the weighty branches causing them to creak and dryly rattle. At the sound she stopped and turned. He'd been there by the tree a moment ago; he'd reached up and caught a branch, plucked an apple and given it to her. She looked at her hands.

Empty.

BIOLOGY, 1969

Miss Monica MacKay was an English teacher and as such
she was possessed of a febrile imagination. Last night, just
before bed she had been marking first year essays on the
Medieval Mystery Plays which the children had illustrated
with the goriest representations of blood and devils she had
ever seen. This had tainted her dreams and now on waking,
she was trying to think of how it would have been to live
in those dark times. How on earth did we survive? And
become so numerous, she wondered. We must be like ants
– rub a few out and the colony will still survive.

She knew that they suffered, did not believe that some
human beings felt more than others, and were more
sensitive to both ends of the spectrum of pain and pleasure,
as had once been believed. But some human beings
certainly showed no evidence of analytical thought; they
just gave way to animal instinct and dropped children as
casually as they dropped litter.

She was a teacher, so she knew.

When, as a young and idealistic woman, she'd imagined
her future pupils, it was her own childhood self she saw;
polite, eager to please, hungry for knowledge, full of awe
for grown-ups (especially teachers), neat and sweet-
smelling. She was aware that ignorance and poverty existed,
but these could be overcome, had been all but overcome.

She was lingering in bed, delaying the moment when
she would rise and, in dressing gown and slippers, make her

way downstairs to the shared bathroom on the first floor. She could not dally too long, she knew, for then her co-tenants in the lodging house, and particularly Mr Peacock, would beat her to the bathroom, throwing her entire day off kilter. Because of this she set her alarm for 5.30 each morning and was bathed and dressed and out of the house by seven.

But lately she'd increasingly grown to dread work.

'Why should I let the toad…' went through her head as she padded along the corridor. Philip Larkin. Hardly a poet the rabble could understand. His language was simple enough, but some of his concepts might be misinterpreted. It was no good explaining that the poem 'Toads' was not an invitation to revolution and anarchy and bunking off school – or as they said here 'mitching'.

She put the plug in the bath and turned on both taps. Checked for a third time that the door was locked and the keyhole covered with a towel, then pulled off her long cotton nightie and dipped one virginal toe in the water. She knelt in three inches of water and sponged herself all over thoroughly, being careful not to wet her hair.

Today she would be teaching 3U, then 1E, then 2E, then she had a free period before lunch. The afternoon was solid; first a very small A level class who were doing Chaucer, then a class of fourteen year olds who, while they were remedial, seemed to enjoy listening to her read *Stig of the Dump*. The last class was 5D, O level English Language; today's subject, comprehension, using the short passage from *Lord of the Flies*, where Piggy's glasses are broken.

'Toads and pigs and flies,' she thought as she sprinkled Bronnley's English Fern talcum powder between her toes. She determined to set her mind on higher matters and begin her day by challenging 3U with some contemporary poetry.

She closed the front door carefully behind her, pleased to find that this late October day greeted her with a clear blue sky and no wind. As usual she glanced back at a house two doors away from her own; Mr Kingsley Amis had once lived there, a lecturer at the university and a published author no less. Not that she had ever met him, except for that one time when he was leaving Mrs Ferguson's, the sweet and tobacco shop, just as she was entering and there had been a sort of tussle of shuffling and to-ing and fro-ing and apologies. It had been nine o'clock on a Saturday morning and he smelled strongly of whisky and tobacco. From the night before, she assumed, though one never knew. The Amis family had moved out of The Grove eight years before, but she so longed for them to return, and so regretted never properly introducing herself, that she always looked wistfully at their house, willing herself back in time or them geographically shifted.

She'd been teaching at the Girls' Grammar back then. The school was temporarily housed in long wooden huts, far too hot in summer and bone chilling in winter. But it had been in a nice part of the town, surrounded by the suburban villas of the middle classes. Due to its ersatz appearance the school's nickname was the cowsheds and she had once, at a dinner-dance, been introduced to someone as one of its 'famous cows'.

When she heard about teaching positions at a new purpose-built school she'd jumped at the opportunity, not knowing that this wonder was to be thrown up on top of a scrubby hill surrounded by a council housing estate on one side and heavy industry and wasteland on the other.

Or that the children attending would be practically feral.

It could drive one quite mad, she thought, a situation like her own.

There was no one at the bus stop when she got there. Not many people about so early in the day. Across the road she noticed a strange woman she had frequently seen in the area. A woman she secretly named Madame de Pompadour. The woman's hair was dyed blue-black and styled in the most astonishing beehive, at least a foot high. Then over the hair, containing it, was a large red chiffon scarf, knotted under her chin. The hairdo was completely out of fashion and would have been outlandish even when it was in fashion, eight or nine years ago. Her make-up was more of a mask than a subtle enhancement; heavily pencilled brows, purple eye shadow, mouth drawn beyond the boundary of its natural size, the scarlet Cupid's bow blurred by the downy hair on her upper lip, tan foundation plastered on, thick and crusted, and then great slaps of rouge on her flaccid cheeks.

She'd witnessed this woman being stared at, laughed at, teased by children, insulted. She also seemed to frighten people with her dead eyes and muttering, which occasionally rose to wild-eyed shrieking when she was provoked too much. Poor woman, Monica thought.

The bus came then and she climbed to the upper deck.

'Why should I let the toad...' she thought, then wondered if she'd said it aloud and glancing around she found a man across the aisle staring at her. Her nervous smile of apology set him on his feet and into the seat next to her.

''ello darling,' he purred, the side of his body pressing into hers. Hot moist breath on her face and neck.

No one else on the top deck. The bus now swaying as it picked up speed and sailed past St James's Church without stopping.

'Excuse me, please,' she said, rising from her seat.

'Alright, darling. No 'urry.' But instead of standing the man merely twisted his legs out into the aisle and as soon as she moved to squeeze past, his hand shot up her skirt, feeling and groping and poking all he found there; her bare skin, stocking tops, suspenders, the elastic of her knickers...

His other hand found her breast, which he squeezed as if it were a fruit he was testing for ripeness.

But she didn't scream.

His feet tangled with hers. Tree branches scraped and thudded the windows on one side of the bus. She nearly fell on him, but managed to wrench herself from his clutches. The last thing he did, quick and sly and stingingly hard, was to slap her retreating bottom and laugh.

She nearly fell down the twisting steps. There on the lower deck all was normal, the bus conductor was sitting and reading the *Daily Mirror* and a cockle-woman, her plump cheeks red with wind-etched veins, a huge wicker basket on her lap, smiled at her.

When the bus stopped at a zebra crossing she stepped off and began to walk back up Mansel Street as fast as she could go without breaking into a run. She kept looking back every few seconds to be certain the man wasn't following her.

The places where he'd touched her were all burning somehow, her breast, her bottom, her private parts. She wanted to rub at them, to rub and rub until his touch was expunged. Yet she also couldn't bear the thought of touching where he'd touched and contaminated her.

Oh, god, why hadn't she screamed? She should have screamed and screamed and clawed at his ugly grinning face.

The bastard, the filthy, filthy, disgusting bastard.

She must get home. Get home and wash herself. Get home and weep with her face pushed into a pillow to smother her cries.

Then she heard her name being called, 'Monica! Monica'.

She slowed and turned, terrified that her assailant was calling her; knew her by name. But instead, there drawn up by the pavement in his green Morris Minor Traveller, was Ken Roberts, Head of Science.

'Hop in. We're holding up the traffic.'

She obeyed, blushing now and trembling.

'You were going the wrong way,' he observed mildly.

'Yes. I thought I'd forgotten a book.'

'Really? Well, just tell me where and I'll turn around.'

'No. No, I … I realise now it's not *The Tempest*. It's not 4I. Not 4E I mean. Not today. I should have checked my diary…' She was talking too much, a stream of gibberish was pouring like mud from her mouth.

'Are you alright?'

'Yes.' The word came out in a croak.

She could not tell him, could not find even the most evasive terms to describe what had happened to her minutes before. She was ashamed. So ashamed. And she had no injuries to show what had happened, no black eye or split lip. She had not screamed.

She felt the man's ragged fingernails scrape at her again. Bile rose at the back of her throat.

'Oh, god! Stop the car! I think I'm going to be sick.'

Ken jammed his foot on the brake and she scrambled out. They were on the road by the North Dock, the Weavers' building seemed to lurch, then jump sideways as she fell onto her hands and knees on the pavement, seized with dry heaving and retching, until at last that morning's tea and toast with marmalade reappeared, little changed in form or colour, but stinking vilely of her digestive fluid.

Her bewildered colleague got out of the car, but uncertain of what to do, merely hovered near the front bumper, a checked brown, yellow and green handkerchief at the ready.

After he'd pulled into the staff car park, he touched her arm.

'My dear, are you quite sure you're up to it? I'm sure we can find someone to drive you home. Apart from anything else, I shouldn't like you to spread a gastric plague amongst the little darlings…' He paused before adding his punch line, 'some of them might quite enjoy it.,.'

She exploded into laughter, then as she tried to restrain it, found that that too was unbearably funny. She saw it briefly in her minds' eye, a nightmare of terrible children green about the gills and spewing and some of them loving the filth of it.

Ken had laughed a little himself at first, pleased that she had understood his dark humour, but his smile faded and he grew embarrassed as she laughed on.

Another vehicle was pulling into the car park, a white Volkswagen Beetle, the Deputy Head's.

Ken got out of the car wanting desperately to distance himself from this hysterical woman. He opened the double back doors of the Morris and, hefting a cardboard box full of exercise books, hissed at her shuddering shoulders and bowed head, 'For god's sake, Miss MacKay! My reputation!' He slammed the door and walked around to the passenger side.

'Morning, Deputy Head!' he called as the Volkswagen's driver emerged.

He opened the passenger door and Monica, ashen-faced, climbed out.

'Could we discuss timetables?' he said to the Deputy Head, who nodded his assent.

Miss MacKay set off for the steps leading to the main entrance. The men fell into step some way behind.

'Is she alright?' Ken asked.

'Miss MacKay? Fine, as far as I know.'

'I see.'

'Bit off was she?'

'Rather, had to stop the car for her to throw up. Between you and me she was acting very oddly.'

'Oh well, shouldn't worry, probably just ... you know, old chap ... women's troubles, time of the month and all that.'

'Biology, you mean.'

'Exactly. Just up your street, Ken, eh? Better prepare the lab and sharpen your scalpel in case of emergency.'

And they laughed, the sound echoing in the empty car park, amplified by the concrete and glass that loomed above them, then falling away into silence.

THE TWICE PRICKED HEART

The Year of Our Lord 1508

So July dawns with an unrepentant sun that blazes down without mercy. The sweating sickness is upon us and strikes with the swiftness of a sword. As if mankind were standing stalks of barley or golden wheat in the field. He who rises in the morning falls down dead at noon and the mother in the very act of setting her sleeping child in his cradle goes to her final rest before he has awoken.

Yet still Margaret's father sits before the fire at dusk retelling his stories. Most familiar is the story of his cockerel shot through the heart by a bolt from a crossbow. This cockerel whom he had named Abel (as when still only a chick he had pecked to death another male chick) was his greatest source of pride. Nothing it seemed could destroy this bird, he had survived no fewer than five raids upon the hen house by a fox, so it was fitting that he should at last submit to death only at the hands and short-sighted vision of the King himself. In recompense her father was paid off with a purse equal to two cocks and ten hens and he presented the King with a dozen eggs and a brown hare.

'Very good meat,' said the King.

'Very good meat,' her father is wont to say. He is a good age her father, past his prime yet still in vigour. Her mother died in childbed not twelve months past and already he is speaking of another wife. She meanwhile cradles her sister in her arms feeding her at intervals with spoonfuls of bread soaked in milk and honey.

Margaret, at fourteen, is the eldest, while Esmerelda, pink-cheeked and fidgeting on her lap is the youngest, being one year old. The others, Edmund, Robert, John, Henry, Jasper, Mary and Martha all died before their second year. And Susanna? Susanna lived to the ripe old age of five and had been her special playmate.

'What of the sailor's eldest?' her father says.

'What of her?'

'Might she not marry soon?'

'Nay, not her. None would have her. She has no dowry save for a spoon carved from whalebone and a shift of sailcloth. Her teeth cross over, one eye has a cast and her bosom is not raised.'

'Yet these are little things are they not? She walks with grace and her hair is golden. She might find a man who looks for obedience and honesty – a man she can be grateful to. Besides, a spoon carved from whalebone is a very fine thing.'

Margaret went and sat at his feet and rested her head upon his knee. 'I am almost grown,' she said. 'I can look after the little one and the house.'

'She showed me that spoon this morning. Her father has sailed to the land of ice, to deserts, to Norway. He's seen whales bigger than a palace, birds that could carry away a grown child in its claws…' His voice trailed off with a sigh and he gazed into the fire as if seeing there everything he'd heard. Margaret looked at him carefully. He seemed less careworn than of late; the melancholy that had ensnared him had dispersed. Her eye fell to his shirt and she noticed a dark spot there. It was his Sunday shirt that he'd put on clean to go to market. She'd have to sponge it before church in two days' time. Her mother would have scolded him and Margaret heard the old words gathering on her tongue, a little army of complaint and scorn. She looked at his face again, so peaceful and gentle, and bit her lip. As if understanding this, he reached down and rested his hand on her head and they sat way for some time in perfect ease and silence.

Three months passed.

The sailor's eldest daughter is now, in law at least, her stepmother. She is meant to replace Margaret's dead mother giving succour and support to her new husband's motherless children. But she is only a year, two at most, older than Margaret and shows no interest, thank God, in mothering her, but equally will have nothing to do with Esmerelda.

'I have been mother to her and *will* be mother to her,' Margaret says in her prayers, partly by way of barter with God.

The sailor's eldest daughter fastens herself to her father's side as a limpet will cling to a rock. She hobbles him with her arms always holding his sleeve or elbow or wrist. Her green eyes fix him in her gaze even with that one eye, her left, aslant.

At night she clings to him; there are sounds and sighs that attest to that. Which is proper for a man and a wife whose union is blessed by God, yet even God's law cannot allow such an excess.

It is an excess that causes the sailor's daughter to lie abed till noon, even when there is work to be done. And there is always work to be done. The sailor's daughter, when she is not eating, or sleeping, sits on the hearth whittling sticks with the knife she keeps in her pocket.

Margaret's father, meanwhile is all smiles; he is as merry as a fool.

So the first months of their marriage pass and while Margaret works as much, if not more, since the arrival of her new mother, she bears it all in good spirits for the sake of her father.

One day in a quiet moment she creeps into her father's bedchamber and takes the whalebone spoon in her trembling hands. Is it a fine thing, this strange instrument? Carved along its length she perceives a number of devilish creatures with bulging eyes and sharp teeth. It is an object of sorcery, a frightening thing. Briskly she puts it back on the ledge where she found it, then without willing them she finds that her hands are wiping themselves on her apron as if befouled.

'If my mother should know of this how she would weep,' she thinks as she sweeps and bakes and feeds the hens and salts the meat and tends to her baby sister.

Esmerelda would not go to her new mother and her new mother seemed blind to the child; once stepping upon her hand as the crawling child crossed her path. She was not deaf to her cries on that occasion, but put her hands over her ears to shut out the sound.

'Take her outside, Margaret,' said her father. 'Her noise is too sharp.'

Margaret dutifully picked up the crying child and took her into the garden and from there into the lane where under the canopy of the trees the light was dappled and blossoms rained upon them like gentle snow in a warming breeze. She kissed her sister's bruised fingers and sang her a lullaby.

In church Margaret often looked at the congregation

and saw many goodly women, some spinsters and others widows who might have gladly married her father. Why did he choose the sailor's daughter?

Winter set in early that year and the earth hardened until it was like iron. Her father said it was time to slaughter the pig, so she set to boiling water and he to sharpening his knife. The sailor's daughter complained of sickness and said she could not mind Esmerelda and could not stand the child's noise, so wrapped in many layers of clothing and a blanket Esmerelda was taken to the yard and set upon a nest of straw on a barrow. The killing of the pig was easily done and Margaret held the bowl to catch the steaming blood, adding a little salt as was always done. The sky was filled with a mass of dense grey-green cloud that blotted out the sun. Together she and her father worked tirelessly, carrying the carcass to the barn where they hung it on the pig spike.

'What was that noise?' he said of a sudden.

'I heard nothing.'

Without another word he rushed back to the house. Margaret went directly to the place where Esmerelda was still sitting quietly. She touched the tip of her sister's nose which was cold, as were her cheeks, but when she placed her hand under her neck to lift her, the child was as warm as a freshly baked pie. Snow began to fall in thick clumps like breadcrumbs as she carried her sister towards the house. Margaret stopped for a moment and looked up at the fast falling snow; she had the sense that she was flying up through it, that each snow flake was held suspended in the icy air as she rushed past them.

Esmerelda, snow settling here and there on her face, stirred and gave a little cry that brought Margaret back to her senses. When she returned to the cottage she saw that her father and stepmother had retired to bed, though it was not yet night.

She put Esmerelda in a chair and the child settled down to sleep as she sang softly to her. The light in the room was made strange by the dark sky and glittering snow. The quiet of the house seemed to swell with each passing second. Margaret sat upon the settle and took up the work basket and began to mend her father's shirt. It was torn under the arm and this she made good before turning it over to inspect it for other signs of wear. She froze at what she saw, for there on the chest where it lay over his heart she found a small puncture hole, the edges of which were stained in a halo of what must be dried blood. She gasped to see this for to her mind such a wound was unlikely to strike the same place twice.

A chill crept over her flesh and looking up she saw that the sun was at the lowest point in the sky and shadows filled the room. Then while she looked about her she saw a movement in the darkest corner of the room that she likened to a moving cloth, such as a woman's cloak, for there was a sort of fluttering wavelike movement to it. Never had she perceived the like before and there was nothing in the room to cast such a shadow.

She kept to her place too terrified to move or make a sound, then just at the moment when she had made up her mind to gather Esmerelda in her arms and flee the house, she heard a step upon the stair and there was the sailor's eldest daughter, dressed in her shift and a wrap, her cheeks aglow, her eyes bright and her lips red and wet and swollen.

'Bring me cheese,' she said, 'and bread and wine.'

Margaret obeyed and cut bread and cheese and filled a

cup with wine for her stepmother, setting them before her with grace.

'Shall my father sup too?' she asked.

The sailor's daughter had filled her mouth with bread and her jaws worked at it energetically. She nodded then lifted the cup to her lips and drank. Some of the wine escaped her lips and dribbled over her chin, down her neck falling onto the collar of her white wrap.

'Shall I call him down to sup? Wake him from his rest?'

The sailor's daughter barely paused except to cram a chunk of cheese in her mouth, then nodded.

Margaret crossed the room pausing to look down on Esmerelda who still slept, her thumb jammed in her mouth, while her shut eyelids rippled with visions from a dream. Then once more from the corner of her eye Margaret thought she saw a grey movement as if someone had stealthily passed by. She shivered and wondered if she was not sickening for an illness, as in a fever the world may seem corrupt and horribly altered.

She went upstairs to her father's chamber and pushed the door open. He lay upon the bed, deep in sleep, his chest bared and his breath so shallow and slow that she scarcely perceived it.

'Father?' she said in a low voice. She crept closer afraid that he would not waken, yet somehow also afraid that he would; for he would be ashamed to be caught there after such lust and idleness. His arms were flung out on either side of him and his palms were open to the heavens, his sinewy fingers curled partly open like the petals of certain wild flowers at dusk.

'Father,' she said again, watching his face intently. Then her gaze drifted to his chest and she saw a small wound over his heart and as she looked a bright red bead of blood appeared and slowly trickled into the gulley at the centre of his chest where it stopped in a narrow pool.

She looked about her as if searching for some other witness to this strange occurrence. Her eye caught sight of the carved whalebone spoon on the ledge where she had last seen it. Its handle had once been round like the blunt head of a seal but now it was a sharp point more like the long beak of a bird and at its tip something red shone wetly as if it had just been dipped in fresh blood.

'Father!' she cried out and shook his shoulder in terror. 'Wake Father, for pity's sake!' She was certain he was dead; murdered by the sailor's daughter with that carved object that was named a spoon but was really an evil device. Made by distant creatures who were ungodly, heathen, misshapen and called Belial, Azazel, Satanail. It was a diabolical thing, capable of puncturing the flesh with swift poison.

'Daughter?' His gentle voice seemed at first distant, as if he were speaking from faraway. 'It is a false voice,' she said to herself, 'Beelzebub can take the guise of the good and make all seem sweet with his tongue.'

'What ails you, child?' He was sitting up in bed, pulling up the covers to hide his naked chest.

She could not speak. It seemed as if her words would go into the air like hooks and all they caught would be sucked back into her throat on an intake of air. She shook her head and turned from him, going on swift feet down the stairs so fast she had the sensation once again that she was flying.

How strange then, how wondrous was the scene in the kitchen, for there sat Esmerelda on her stepmother's lap, her laughing face uplifted, cheeks plump and glowing, her eyes bright and dancing. There is such music in a child's burbling giggle it lifts the heart, she thought, and wondered at it. Moments before she had been cast down and full of fear. She had judged the sailor's daughter to be selfish and indolent and dangerous, now she saw how the false mother dandled her stepchild on her knee and laughed and smiled and fed her currants.

You should be happy, Margaret said to herself, this is what you yearned for and now the happy day has arrived. Yet a greater fear stirred in her agitated heart which could be likened to the moment cream becomes butter and its elemental nature is entirely changed and can never be changed back. Her fear was that of a deposed king – she would be toppled from her rightful place and neither love nor consideration nor obedience would anymore be hers.

Her father came downstairs and stood at the stair door hearty as a king with his hands on his hips, stopping to feast his eyes on the domestic harmony before him.

'And what have we here? A pretty sight indeed!'

Silently and almost unseen Margaret crossed the room, lifted the latch on the door and stepped outside.

The yard was quiet, and made strange by the snow that covered everything. *I must make my own way in the world*, she thought, and turning, meaning to go back into the house, she perceived a figure stepping from behind the high hedge in the lane. He was wrapped in a grey cloak that mingled with the deep shade under the trees. Only his face showed white, his domed brow, black eyes and blacker eyebrows, his long nose and grey streaked beard. She knew him at once; it was the sailor.

He stepped towards her, the snow creaking underfoot, half of his face was smiling, but only half for an old wound had paralysed the right side and a long silvery scar marked his cheek from the corner of his mouth to his ear.

'So you are his eldest girl, then?' he said.

She nodded and gestured for him to follow her into the house.

'There's time yet,' he said. She frowned wondering at his meaning.

'I have been to places you wouldn't dream of. Seen things beyond the world's telling. And this,' he said, 'I brought for you.' From under his cloak he took an object that glowed white and was as slender as Margaret's forearm. It was like the whalebone spoon that had so entranced her father, but smaller. 'See here now, girl, there's a leaping stag and here a lizard, there a running hare!'

She took it reluctantly from his outstretched hand, sensing trickery.

'My poor wife died these five weeks past,' he said and clasped her hand. 'Like your poor mother was taken from thee. His wife from him.' He nodded towards the house. 'So now there is a tally to be made. One for one is fair exchange and the empty ship needs ballast.'

Understanding at last his meaning she pulled away violently, drawing both her hands back and, without thinking, sharply pulling the tip of the carved spoon to her breast.

'Oh!' she cried, for she felt a sharp pain. She looked down at the place on her apron over her heart and saw a tiny spot of blood; dark and small as if an insect had alighted there.

'That's once,' he said and, leaning forward, kissed her.

THE FLOWER MAKER

Amanda was nine years old. She lived with her mama and papa in an apartment on the Rue St Denis. Mama, Papa, little mouse, Amanda and her collection of beautiful German dolls. It was 1940. Mama wasn't well. She had a bad head and lay most days in the shuttered room at the end of the hall. The door was always closed. Their maid, Julienne, came every morning to clean the house and wash their clothes and to tell Amanda that she was a very bad girl, a spoiled girl. But Amanda tried hard to be good. She whispered, she tiptoed so that she wouldn't wake Mama. She never made a mess, was careful not to scatter crumbs when she ate her bread and she folded her clothes and put them away in the dresser when it was time to go to bed.

As it was the Christmas vacation and Mama was still not well and Papa had to go to his office, Amanda spent most of her time alone in her room. From her window she watched Monsieur Arbot across the way. As the weather was wintry and dark, even in the middle of the day, he had the gaslight on in his little shop. There were not so many flowers then, because it was winter, because of the war.

Lately he had been selling flowers made of tiny scraps of fabric; the silk and satin and tulle of long-ago ball gowns, the silvery slippery linings of expensive coats and jackets. Amanda had seen a dark-haired woman go in there once, twice, sometimes three times a week. She carried a large loose package wrapped in newspaper and string. And

178

although the parcel was big it was easy to see that it was light; like a piece of imprisoned air. The woman had a face that was very narrow and pale, with a small pointed nose and big eyes with dark shadows under them. She did not have a winter coat, just an old shapeless jacket that she pulled tight around her thin body. She wore black lace-up shoes, no stockings and no socks either. On her head she tied a woollen scarf that might have once been red, but was now faded to a mucky uneven pink.

If Monsieur Arbot had a customer inside the shop she waited outside, hugging her newspaper package and moving from one foot to the other as if the pavement burned the soles of her feet. When the customer had gone, she went inside and laid her bundle on the counter, then crossed her arms over her chest and hugged herself. Monsieur Arbot stood opposite her on the other side of his counter; he had a small paraffin stove back there and stayed near it for most of the day. Carefully, he unwrapped the package the woman had brought, opening it out so that the artificial flowers lay in a loose bunch before him. Usually, when that was done, he would get a white bowl from the shelf and fill it with steaming coffee from the pot he kept on top of his stove. He put it on the counter top, then nodded at it, which was the cue for the woman to pick it up. She wrapped both hands around it.

Amanda decided that she would ask her papa for a few copper coins so that she could buy some of the flowers. Amanda, although she was only nine years old, sensed in a barely understood way that she wanted possession of two or three of those strange flowers so that she could understand better the woman who made them, and understand too Monsieur Arbot, and the shortage of real flowers and everything beyond that; everything that seems to radiate outwards from the little flower shop with its soft gas light that turned the snow on the pavement outside yellow.

'Papa, please can I have some money, so that I can buy Mama a present to cheer her up?'

Papa smiled, though Amanda could see that sadness hid somewhere on his face – perhaps it was in his eyes, or in the set of his shoulders. He leaned to one side in the winged armchair by the fire, lifting one hip so that he could reach into his pockets for the loose change he kept there.

'May I go tomorrow? May I tell Julienne you said I might?' She was excited now, and wanted time to fly away; for the hands on all the clocks to suddenly give up their slow, barely perceptible progress and spin faster and faster until it was morning.

'Yes, yes,' he said and patted her warm little face which he found to be as soft and smooth as the delicate skin on the inside of a woman's thigh. 'Yes, tell Julienne I said you could go.'

The next day Julienne grudgingly unlocked the apartment door and watched as Amanda disappeared down the stairs to the street.

There was very little traffic in that part of the town; the odd automobile, sometimes an army truck, a horse-drawn carriage or a hand wagon pulled slowly by tired country people

Amanda crossed the street and when she reached the pavement outside the florist's she turned to look for her window in the apartment block opposite. She saw it almost straight away even though there were many windows. Her curtains were red, the brightest red there was. She had picked them herself; back before Mama got so sick.

Before she'd left her room Amanda had put her favourite doll on the window ledge facing out so that the doll could watch her. She saw her doll standing behind the glass, with the red curtains on either side, and remembered the ballet she had gone to see when she was little, *Coppelia*. Amanda waved at the doll, wishing, but also fearing, that the doll would wave back. She didn't, of course, but Amanda felt glad to sense the doll's eyes watching her; nothing could hurt her as long as the doll was there. Or at least if something did happen, if the soldiers or a perhaps a monster came and stole Amanda away, then at least the dolls would know. They wouldn't think she had abandoned them.

Thus satisfied, the little girl turned her attention to the display in Monsieur Arbot's brightly lit window. The snow had almost gone; only grey dirty heaps remained in dark places hidden from the sun.

She stood looking carefully at the tall metal buckets that held the real flowers as well as the flowers that had been made from fabric. The ledge of the shop, now that she was at street level, hid from view the other side of the counter where Monsieur Arbot warmed himself and where he kept brown paper, string, thin wire and a wooden cash box.

Amanda pushed open the door to the shop and entered. Monsieur Arbot looked up at the sound of the door and at first wore an expression of bewilderment as he had expected to see a customer at eye level with him.

'*Bonjour Monsieur Arbot*,' Amanda said politely, remembering how her mama had always addressed shopkeepers.

'Oh,' he said, '*Bonjour Mademoiselle*.' But he didn't smile, merely gazed at the child blankly.

'I want to buy some flowers. For my mama, as she is sick.'

He grunted miserably in response and flapped his hand

both inviting her to get on with her errand and dismissing the child at the same time.

Amanda went to inspect the artificial flowers first. The ones inside the shop were somewhat forlorn, the fabrics used to make these were dull; brown tweeds and grey and dark-blue gabardine. As objects they still possessed some charm, but lacked the bright triumphant beauty of the ones in the window. Amanda was surprised by this and now understood why only the best ones with the richest fabrics took pride of place in the window.

She went to look at these next and saw with delight that not only were they just as beautiful close up as they had seemed from afar, but the different fabrics of each leaf and petal brought back distant memories of life before the war, before her mama became ill. The flower-printed crepe, the shiny sky-blue satin, the baby-pink silk and paisley swirls and deep red velvets and gold brocades all seemed to conjure school friends' parties and her mother's and aunt's beautiful ball gowns and shawls.

Amanda glanced up at her bedroom window once more and saw her doll on the ledge between the curtains. She wondered which flowers took the doll's interest, but as she could not tell the precise direction of the glass-eyed gaze, Amanda resorted to make-believe, and imagined the doll was staring pointedly at four pink and white flowers which had been arranged on their own in a small cone-shaped container near the window.

'Monsieur?' said Amanda, 'how much are those, please?'

'Which? Ah, the tea roses, let me see, how much money do you have to spend?'

Amanda stepped up to the sales desk and emptied her purse on its surface. The coins scattered and spilled, most of them a dirty dark brown colour, not bright and coppery like new ones.

Monsieur Arbot slid them one by one rapidly across the surface of the desk and into his palm, counting under his breath as he did so.

He smiled at last.

'Well, my child, you have only enough for three and a half of those flowers, but as today I am in a good mood I will let you have four.'

He dropped the coppers into the concealed drawer. Amanda heard the sound of its mechanism open, then the tinkle and patter of coins as they fell inside the wooden drawer and the smart click as it was closed again.

She knew him so well. Knew how he half crouched behind the counter in order to eat his bread and sausage, then quickly wiped his hands and mouth with a big white handkerchief when customers came in. She knew how he scratched his behind and sometimes dozed off with his head resting on his arm until he was jolted awake by a sudden noise. She knew how he conducted his transactions with the maker of the fabric flowers with hardly a word passing between them, how he was kind to the poor dark-haired woman and gave her coffee so that she might warm herself.

He came out from behind the counter and lifted the container of flowers from the window, holding them aloft so that she could see them and acknowledge that those were the ones she had wanted.

He went behind the counter again, as she knew he would.

'I have no brown paper, so will newspaper do?' he asked.

Amanda nodded, sensing a lie.

Indeed later, once Amanda was back in her room, she

looked down into Monsieur Arbot's shop and saw clearly that he did have a roll of brown paper and that he used it freely with his other customers.

But other dramas would play out first, as while Monsieur was tying a short loop of string around the stems of the bouquet, the door to the shop opened and the flower maker herself entered.

It was the woman's habit, Amanda knew, never to enter the shop when the florist had customers to attend to, but here she was, hesitant and pale, her lips a strange unnatural bluish red, her hair lifeless and flat (reminding Amanda of a drowned rat she had once found by the side of a flooded sewer).

Amanda guessed that the woman hadn't seen the small child in the shop, hidden as she was by the window ledge and the pots of flowers.

The woman came forward quickly and seemed barely to register Amanda as she neared the counter. She concentrated intensely on Monsieur Arbot; her eyes, Amanda noticed, were darkly circled and the whites were stained pale yellow just like the snow outside the lit shop window at twilight. Amanda felt both fascination and pity for the woman. There was ugliness in the eyes and the pallid skin; her hands were red, dry and sore looking and the intricate mechanisms of the bones beneath the thin skin showed through yellow-white like chicken bones.

If the woman failed to notice Amanda, Monsieur Arbot now chose to ignore the child. Amanda stood near the counter holding her wrapped bouquet of pink and white satin flowers before her like a bridesmaid.

The woman placed a new package of flowers on the counter for the florist's inspection. He poured her a bowl

184

of coffee. Amanda noticed how her hands trembled as she took it and lifted it to her mouth, clattering the lip of the bowl against her teeth at first, and then drinking noisily. Neither the woman nor Monsieur Arbot had yet spoken.

He opened the package, but on seeing its contents clucked his tongue in disapproval. The woman continued to suck at the coffee, drawing it into her mouth greedily. Amanda stole a glance at the flowers and saw with disappointment that these were the dull-coloured woollen ones.

Monsieur Arbot did not open his change drawer, did not scoop up a dirty handful of coppers, did not tenderly place the new flowers in the window display. Instead he retied the package and shook his head slowly.

The woman was so engrossed in drinking the coffee that she didn't at first notice what was happening, but when the rejected flowers were pushed back to her side of the counter, she quickly grew alarmed and began to speak rapidly in a language Amanda did not understand. Perhaps Monsieur Arbot understood, but whether or not he did, he was unmoved, his head a metronome, slowly turning from side to side.

The woman jabbered; her voice, which was husky and strained, grew shrill. She put her hands together palm to palm, praying and pleading, her eyes ever wider, her brow a knot of anguish. He tried to ignore the woman, then angrily, desperate to break the spell of her noise, he banged the heel of his fist on the centre of the wooden worktop, and shouted, *'Non!'*

Both the woman and Amanda jumped at the sudden noise, but it had done its work. The woman bit her lip and picked up the loose package. Then just as she turned to go the florist groaned and uttered a curse, and called briskly,

'Madame!'

She turned and he tossed three coins in her direction. They fell at her feet and she quickly picked up two, but the third was nearer to Amanda.

The child stepped forward, bending to retrieve the coin, and as she did so she met the woman's gaze for the first time. They stared at one another for a moment, then stood up. Amanda, holding her bouquet upside-down, dangling the four satin flower heads like the hanged man on a tarot card, lifted her other hand towards the woman, the small copper coin held between her thumb and forefinger. The woman stared at her in confusion for a moment and then, bobbing her head briefly, quickly took the coin and left the shop.

Amanda followed. The woman, once she was a few paces from the shop, hesitated as if uncertain which way to go. She seemed distressed, her head turning this way and that, while her feet remained fixed to that one slab of pavement.

Amanda went to her side.

'Madame?' she said and reached for the woman's hand, which was cold to the touch and made Amanda think about the ivory soap dish on the washstand in her mama's bedroom.

The woman looked at Amanda. Her expression was one of incomprehension; frowning, she shook her head at the child.

Amanda lifted her bouquet of flowers the right way up; the hanged man restored to buoyant and rude health.

'Oh,' the woman said, and touched the petals of one of the flowers, smoothing the pink satin between her fingers as if measuring its quality.

Amanda would remember this gesture all her life; her

upraised arm, how small she must have been then, and yet how strong and generous she felt. But Amanda was also aware then, as later, that she didn't quite know what she was doing, what she meant to happen. Did she mean to give these flowers to the woman so that she could take them and sell them once again to Monsieur Arbot? Or was she communicating something else to the woman, something about her appreciation of the woman's talent, of the beauty of the flowers. Or perhaps a meaning which was even greater; a reminder of happy days, of beauty, of life?

But the woman did not take the flowers from Amanda's outstretched arm; instead she suddenly withdrew her hand, turned her back and hurried away. Amanda watched her go, saw how her shoulders were hunched against the bitter cold of the sunless morning, and she grew aware of the frost that crept up through the soles of her boots, chilling her to the bone.

THE MOON AND THE BROOMSTICK

There had been three, perhaps four miscarriages already. Two had happened when Maria's pregnancy was already far advanced.

The midwife examined her hips, her teeth, the taut muscles of her stomach.

She was treated like a naughty girl. Ordered, now she was pregnant again, to give up all violent exercise. Maria's mother, the Russian acrobat and contortionist, Tatiana Britt had never abandoned her calling – practising her skills behind the scenes when she became too unwieldy to perform for the public.

But she dearly wanted a child, and so at winter's end when she was five months pregnant she bid farewell to Stan (or the Great Bendini as he was publicly known) when he left to begin the season with the travelling circus.

She felt lonely and bored, but spent hours at a time resting with her feet propped up so they were higher than her head. She wrote Stan long letters asking after all their friends, mentioning the small towns that she knew they would be going to, reminding him of things they had once done together, telling him she loved him. He replied twice. His letters were concise.

But Maria was grateful for all the benefits modern medicine had bestowed. It was a young century, the atlas still sported many splashes of pink to show that Britannia held onto her empire, and scientific progress had transformed the lives of many.

Children no longer worked in the mines or factories, fewer women died in childbirth, though there was still a very real risk. And babies and children, even once safely delivered, might yet die from any number of causes.

Guiltily then, she ignored her impatience and boredom, and submitted to examinations and thermometers and bed rest.

The sheets on her bed in the nursing home were starched white cotton, crisp and cool, the food was bland and luke-warm, and she had been disallowed not only brandy, which she liked to take a lick of now and then throughout the day, but also coffee as it was thought to induce miscarriage by quickening the heart.

Tea was offered instead and she grew to like it well enough, but it was a pale substitute.

Her belly ballooned; so much so that she was cross-examined about her dates, about her monthlies and marital relations with Stan. When she told the nurse that she and Stan were intimate frequently, once or twice a day, some-times in the afternoon, and even, shockingly, during her menses, the nurse's face grew ashen and she looked as if she might faint. When the nurse had recovered, she said that this was *unnatural*, a woman's body was not designed for such overuse and he, Stan, must learn self-control and shouldn't make her suffer so.

'But it isn't suffering,' she'd protested, 'I like it.'

The nurse shook her head slowly in reproach.

'But my dear, you've lost four babies. Don't you see?'

Maria saw.

Next they accused her of overeating.

'Mother must eat for two, but she must not overindulge.'

Finally they began to suggest that she might be carrying

twins, and searched her belly, pressing the stethoscope first here, then there to detect a second or third heartbeat.

By her seventh month she was instructed to prepare her nipples for breast-feeding, something that she could not understand but endured. She was given, as were all the expectant mothers, a small nail brush and a bar of disinfectant soap and instructed to scrub her nipples twice a day. It was painful but she did as she was told, marvelling at how women in more primitive countries, or in the past, or Eve herself, mother of Cain and Abel, had managed to procure a nailbrush and carbolic. How had the human race managed to survive and thrive without? Well, she considered, perhaps something was done with bunches of twigs and herbs?

Then she began to imagine her twins (which by the rough and tumble that went on in her belly she was convinced must be boys) tasting the carbolic soap on her nipples when she first offered suck, and pulling nasty faces before refusing her delicious milk. So secretly, a month before they were due, she stopped using the soap and after one week of grating the wet brush on her weary nipples, she abandoned that too.

Stan wrote saying that they should name the boys Romulus and Remus, and included a diagram of a she-wolf he'd had the idea of constructing. Concealed inside the animal's teats were two baby's bottles filled with cow's milk. He was always coming up with new and wild ideas for the circus and while she could see the appeal of this one, she didn't think it would work, not for her two boys anyway; and she suggested that perhaps it would be better performed by dwarves in diapers?

But the names were nice enough, and they could always give the boys a whole clutch of others so that they could decide later on which to use in their act, which for friends and family and which for the world beyond the circus. So, Romulus Samson Jacob John and Remus Nero Alexander Harold grew in her imagination, not weighted down by their freight of names, but strong, agile, handsome and clever boys who would become great men.

Two weeks before the babies were due, another woman was brought onto the ward. Like Maria, this woman was expecting twins. Her belly was prodigious and vast, her insect legs and arms tiny in comparison, her small pale face fearful and timid as a mouse's.

She was a vicar's wife, as devout as a nun. She called out for God's help in a choked whisper between bouts of weeping. Her labour had begun thirty-six hours before in the vicarage, a long and rackety drive away from the hospital. The babies were stuck and despite all the manipulation and coaxing from the midwife they would not budge. In a few hours, if natural childbirth did not occur, the babies, dead or alive, would be removed by Caesarean section. If not, mother and babies would be lost.

They wheeled the woman off at close to midnight, her cries echoing down the tiled passage, 'Oh God, oh God, oh Jesus, Jesus.'

Perhaps the same thing would happen to her, for Maria surmised, if God punished and tested even the virtuous vicar's wife, what might he do to her; an unvarnished sinner who had only jumped the broomstick with her Stan, and not legally married in God's eyes.

She lay in bed terrified for what seemed like hours. Waves of spasmodic pain were passing through her body. It was two weeks too early, but it was now, and now was implacable, irresistible; she couldn't fight it. She struggled to sit upright, the twins seemed locked in a tight knot of stillness in a different, lower position in her body. Her eyes travelled up the ward to the desk where the night nurse usually sat in a quiet pool of yellow light, passing the dark hours by reading romantic novels or knitting Argyle sweaters for her sweetheart, but there was no one there.

Four other women slept in the other beds, all of them heaped on their sides, bulky as sows under the covers.

She swung her legs over the side of the bed and struggled to stand. A contraction overtook her and she waited it out, rubbing her back to ease the pain and rocking her body like an Arabian dancer because that seemed to help, but was probably forbidden.

Slowly, as every four or five minutes another contraction stopped her, she made her way towards the door that led out of the ward and closer to the delivery rooms. It was hot and airless, and despite the strong smells of disinfectant she could detect the coppery tang of blood in the air.

She heard voices up ahead, words spoken in urgent whispers, and these seemed to be coming from a lit room whose door was ajar describing its edges with a sharp shape of white light.

Another contraction overtook her and she stopped near an open door. Resting one hand on the doorjamb to steady herself, she undulated heavily, sensing weakness in her once strong legs that must have come from underuse. She wished that she could be with Stan; that instead of being here in this distempered place with its imprisoning walls, she could be in their little wooden caravan, breathing in the smells of the animals, the axle grease and the sweet, sweet air.

She gazed into the unlit room and noticed the silvery disk that hung beyond the window. It was a full, round moon with a hazy halo of light around it. She thought about Stan sitting on the caravan steps with his pipe, how he would look up and see this same moon. As soon as this idea came to her she felt she must get nearer to that moon, to stand by the window and press her hot cheek against the cool glass. If she thought hard enough and gazed intently enough at the moon, it would be as if Stan were with her and he would know that she was thinking of him.

She knew that it was forbidden to trespass into any room other than the bathroom, yet could not resist. She had gone forward only two steps when her stomach tightened again and a great wave of pain paralysed her. The rocking seemed to help, if only to focus her mind on something other than the burning cramped ache that coiled through her. There was no wall to support herself by, but her hand, groping in the gloom, found a metal rung, probably part of a bed, which she wrapped her trembling fist around.

When the contraction had passed (they were getting longer as well as more intense and closer together) she stepped forward still holding onto the metal rail. Now that she was closer to the window she stepped into the pool of its pale silver light, and she saw that what she had been holding was the foot of a metal crib, and inside it she saw two perfect babies' heads laying next to one another on the mattress. A single white sheet lay over the babies and their tiny eyes were closed. She leaned closer, holding her belly as she did so. She did not think she had ever seen anything so perfect as these alabaster babies with blue veined eyelids, and long black lashes and mouths so pale and perfectly formed. She immediately sensed that they were not breathing and thus not alive, but something about them convinced her that they weren't dead – or at least not dead in the way that something which has once been alive is dead. No, she had a barely formed impression that these were dolls.

Or not dolls as such, but something like. Perhaps they were wax or bisque mannequins used for the purpose of training the doctors or other scientific research.

Another contraction and she gripped the sides of the crib and swayed. Again the pain drifted away, retreating from body and mind momentarily and leaving behind the surprising nothingness of no pain.

She looked at the baby mannequins again. It seemed both strange and frustrating to her that someone had lain them in this crib and covered them with a sheet just as if they were asleep. You'd think they'd be kept in a cupboard or under glass, not put to bed like a little girl's dolls.

Without thinking about it (as after all these were not real babies; they would not get cold and die) she drew back the sheet, and that was when she saw it, saw the strangeness of what had been done to the tiny naked mannequins. They were joined together. It was as if the wax or whatever they were made from had been allowed to melt and pool, fusing their lower torsos together into one unnatural trunk.

They were girls, and each had a clamped stump at her belly button and an elusive odour, sweet and sour at the same time. It was that which made her realise that they were real – not mannequins at all. She gasped and would have stepped back, but another contraction locked her in place, and she thought with terror of the violence inside her and she was suddenly more afraid than she had ever been. She who had soared through the air, somersaulting, balancing, or hanging by a leather strap in her teeth while her body spun beneath her, a cocoon of weight like a plumb bob.

She screamed. The sound was low, guttural and strangled, and the noise seemed to come from somewhere else entirely, as if it was the echo of another woman's voice, another woman's pain.

And then as if in answer to her cry, she felt a sudden hot gush as her waters broke, and voices and people surrounded her. Hands were on her body pulling her away and out of the moonlit room, but the grip of her hands on the crib's rail was so strong that it jerked and rattled, shaking the wax babies so it seemed for a moment that they might wake. Alarmed, she let go and the crib clanked heavily and was still.

Her twins were also girls. Black-haired and button-eyed, with faces like fairy changelings, and perfect, perfect, perfect.

She made a promise to the moon the next night. She and Stan would marry. She'd been warned; she did not know what sin the vicar's wife, poor thing, was guilty of, but from now on Maria decided she must make amends.

Stan would understand. He invented the world as he went along; nothing was beyond him.

For years after, especially when the moon was full, she saw again the poor dead babies with their fused bodies and blue white skin and sometimes she thought she'd dreamt it all. Or worse it occurred to her that the dead twins had been *her* babies, and these two bright girls, Charlotte-Kay and Georgina-May were the children of the vicar and his good wife, and somehow, by unnatural chance or charm, she'd stolen them.

And later still, when times were hard, and Stan told her of his latest plan, she saw the rightness of it straight away.

She sensed that it had almost been the girls' fate to be Siamese twins, and now with tiny corsets stitched together at the hip and tiny beautifully made little double dresses, it became their destiny, and no one, not even their mother thought it was a sin.

UNDONE, 1969

The girls have sewing class. The boys, metalwork, carpentry, technical drawing.

The first task in sewing is to make an apron.

While from the mysterious workroom of the carpentry class with its resin scent of wood, its hammers and vices, boys sometimes appear bearing the fruits of their labour. Curious objects these, darkly varnished; a block on a stand with a shelf into which small crenullations have been cut. A pipe rack.

When they are grown, these girls, these boys, father will select a pipe, fill it with tobacco, tamp it down, then sit in his armchair before he lights it. Mother comes in then, hen-like and hesitant, a steaming cup of tea trembling on its matching saucer. She is wearing the gingham apron she sewed ten years ago when she was twelve.

That is the picture, as nice and clean as the images in the Ladybird books. To this they aspire.

Or should.

Except.

This one, knee socks sagging, the elastic in their tops exhausted, snapped white filaments escaping like stray hairs. This one, needle and thread in hand, tries to form the long tacking stitches as she has been instructed, but fails. She takes it up to the teacher for her inspection.

'No. No. The line is not straight. The stitches are uneven. Unpick it. Start again.'

Some of the other girls sit at the prow of the sewing machines, pressing their black-shod feet on the foot pedal, nudging the engine into stuttering buzzing life.

They are the chosen.

Back at her table she snips the knot from the cotton. Pulls out the thread of her morning. Has barely rethreaded the needle before the bell rings.

Next week is the same as last week. Here are the same two pieces of gingham, limper now than when she began. Here is the needle with its length of cotton. Another knot is tied. Here is the needle going into the same hole as last week.

'No,' the teacher says. 'Start again.'

Another week. Weary now. This is a glass mountain. This is spinning straw into gold. Impossible. More girls are graduating to the sewing machines. One is standing by the mirror as the teacher ties the apron in a bow around her waist. Both beam with happiness.

Why do her stitches misbehave? To her they look straight enough, even enough and once the seam has been fed through the machine these temporary stitches will be removed and forgotten.

Where is Rumpelstiltskin when you need him?

This is her fate forever.

Charles Lamb's sister Mary was a mantua maker, stabbing her needle in, her needle out, in the dying, desperate winter light. Then one day she stitched her mother with a knife.

It is quite possible to drive a woman mad with too much stitching.

Next to her at the sewing table is Jane Thomas. Jane Thomas has just turned thirteen. She has black shiny hair, sallow skin, brown eyes. She is sturdily built with breasts already evident under her grey pullover.

Jane is whispering urgently, telling unbidden tales of her life to her pale childlike companion.

'I went with Shalto Davies last night,' she hisses. 'We went around the back of the club and he…'

The words that followed were graphic, crude, shocking. They described an intimacy. An exploration of … with … not his 'thing' but a finger.

'And he said I had a … like a…'

The last word was astonishing.

Metaphors. They had studied them.

A cloud like cotton wool.

Green as grass.

It was the 'c' word the girl said he had used.

Can these be the words of love? The true words of love and not the ones in all the pop songs sung by those spangle-eyed boys.

Love, love me do. Pretty woman. Young girl.

And what metaphor pray, did her ardent suitor employ? What velvety flower; pink and secret? What bee-kissed bud, its unopened petals damp with dew?

The needle goes in, comes out. No wonder her line of stitching is uneven, erratic.

Q. Why is virginity like a balloon?

A. One prick and it's gone!

She doesn't yet understand jokes like that. Yes, prick a balloon and it explodes into withered shreds, but the rest is mysterious.

Jane is delighted by the story she is telling. Thrilled.

So what was the metaphor?

'Bucket.'

Cold. Hard. Capacious. Rattling. Tinny. Empty. Rhymes with…

At the pantomime a month ago, a thin sorry-looking man and his monstrous outsized wife performed a duet.

'There's a hole in my bucket,

Dear Liza, dear Liza …'

'Well, fix it!

Dear Henry, dear Henry!'

Who shall we be when we are grown? Where are our role models?

Even then, in her startling innocence and ignorance, Jane's words didn't sound right. She kept her eyes on the fabric, raw edges fraying from too much handling, listening to her friend who is boastful, proud of this summation of a secret part of her anatomy.

A mantua maker could never quite earn enough to make ends meet. Often she was forced to resort to the streets and prostitution.

Unpick that.

Start again.

And again.

On into infinity. Never finish the row of tacking, never graduate to the sewing machine, never complete that gingham apron. Fail at everything.

But listen. Listen.

Flowers, leaves, branches all reach for the sun. Nothing ends yet. It may be only the beginning.

About the Author

Jo Mazelis is a novelist, short-story writer and essayist. Her collection of stories *Diving Girls* (Parthian, 2002) was short-listed for the Commonwealth Best First Book and Wales Book of the Year Awards. Her second book, *Circle Games* (Parthian, 2005), was longlisted for Welsh Book of the Year. Her first novel *Significance* (Seren, 2014) was a winner of the Jerwood Fiction Uncovered Award in 2015. Jo was born in Swansea where she currently lives. Originally trained at Art School, she worked for many years in London in magazine publishing as a freelance photographer, designer and illustrator, including on *Spare Rib* and *City Limits*, before studying for an MA in English Literature. She has had numerous short stories in anthologies and listed for awards, including five shortlistings for the Rhys Davies short-story prize. Several of her stories have been broadcast on Radio 4.

Acknowledgements

'Caretakers' was published in *The Wish Dog* (Honno), 'Mechanics' will be published in *Eto* in 2016, 'The Murder Stone' appeared in *Litro*, 'Word Made Flesh' was published by *Wales Arts Review*, 'Velvet' in *Southword*, 'The Green Hour' in *The Lonely Crowd*, 'Storm Dogs' in *A Flock of Shadows* (Parthian), 'Mrs Dundridge' and 'The Flower Seller' in *Eagle in the Maze* (Cinnamon Press) 'Levitation, 1969' in *New Welsh Short Stories* (Seren), 'Whose Story is this Anyway?' and 'The Twice Pricked Heart' in *The Lonely Crowd,* 'The Moon and the Broomstick' in *Sing Sorrow Sorrow* (Seren).

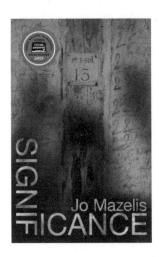

Significance

by Jo Mazelis

Pb £9.99
Seren 2014
ISBN: 9781781722930

Winner of the **Jerwood Fiction Uncovered prize** 2015

'With *Significance* Mazelis has set her novel-writing bar at a breathtaking height.' – Rachel Trezise, *Agenda*

Lucy Swann is trying on a new life. She's cut and dyed her hair and bought new clothes, but she's only got as far as a small town in northern France when her flight is violently cut short. When Inspector Vivier and his handsome assistant Sabine Pelat begin their investigation, the chance encounters of her last days take on a new significance.

Lucy's death, like a stone thrown into a pool, sends out far-reaching ripples, altering the lives of people who never knew her as well as those of her loved ones back home.